"Is there still something between you and your ex?"

"Are you kidding?" Piper's grimace, complete with eyes rounded in horror, did Josh's heart good. "He's one of the reasons I need boyfriend camouflage this weekend."

"Oh." Josh glanced at the doorway, noting that he and Piper were visible to anyone in the dining room. "And your grandmother's fondest dream is to see you in the arms of a good man, right?" *Don't do it.*

"Right."

He took a step toward her. Maybe he shouldn't do this, but how could just once hurt? "I have an idea that should make your grandmother ecstatic."

Piper's ocean-colored eyes grew so wide he could drown in them. She stood on tiptoe to meet him, and then his lips were on hers.

Fire raced in his blood. Too late he realized that the reality of kissing her was far more devastating to his senses than the fantasy, and his assumption that he could walk away from "just one" kiss unaffected had been foolish.

Still, as long as he was making the mistake, he should make the most of it.

Dear Reader,

One of the fun parts of my job is exploring the different ways two people can end up together. As much as I love stories about a man and a woman who make an instant connection, I'm a sucker for stories about people who start out as friends. People who don't immediately realize (or want to admit) what's right in front of them, so they try in vain to fight the attraction. But the sexual tension and emotional undercurrent can't be ignored.

At least, that's the case for my heroine, Piper Jamieson, and her best friend, Josh Weber. Career-driven Piper has no time for romance in her life, especially not with a heartbreaker like Josh. When she needs a date for the weekend, though, her sexy best friend fills in—with unexpected results.

Piper and Josh are very special to me, maybe because I married my own best friend, maybe because they were just so much fun to write. I hope you enjoy their story and will check out the information about my other books and my story-themed giveaways at www.mindspring.com/~tjmic.

Happy reading!

Tanya

Books by Tanya Michaels

HARLEQUIN DUETS
96—THE MAID OF DISHONOR

HARLEQUIN FLIPSIDE
6—WHO NEEDS DECAF?

TANYA MICHAELS

HERS FOR THE WEEKEND

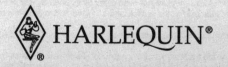

HARLEQUIN®

TORONTO • NEW YORK • LONDON
AMSTERDAM • PARIS • SYDNEY • HAMBURG
STOCKHOLM • ATHENS • TOKYO • MILAN • MADRID
PRAGUE • WARSAW • BUDAPEST • AUCKLAND

With special thanks to Jennifer Green
for believing in me and my characters.

ISBN 0-373-69168-8

HERS FOR THE WEEKEND

1

PIPER JAMIESON SAGGED against the sofa cushions and rolled her eyes at the phone receiver. It could have been a wrong number, a pushy telephone solicitor, an obscene caller even, but nooo, it was her mother. Piper loved her mom, but all their conversations boiled down to the same argument—Piper's love life.

She started to put her feet up on the oval coffee table, but stopped suddenly, as though her mother could see through the phone line and into her apartment. "So, how've you been doing, Mom?"

"Never mind that. I'm more concerned with how *you* are," her mother said. "You don't feel acute appendicitis coming on, right? You aren't going to call us tomorrow with a severe case of forty-eight-hour east Brazilian mumps or something?"

Piper groaned. Although she'd bailed out on all of the family reunions in recent years, she'd used legitimate work-related excuses, never fictional medical ones. But this year she'd made a promise to her grandmother.

This year, there would be no reprieve.

"I'll be there," she assured her mother. "And I'm looking forward to seeing you all." *Mostly.*

"We're looking forward to seeing you, too, honey. Especially Nana. When I went to visit her at the hospital last week—"

"Hospital?" Piper's chest tightened. She adored her grandmother, even if Nana did stubbornly insist women needed husbands. "Daphne told me she was under the weather, but no one said anything about the hospital." As Nana advanced in years, Piper couldn't help worrying over her grandmother's health.

A worry her mother was not above exploiting. "You know what would help your Nana? If she knew you had a good man to take care of you."

Ah, yes—here came the Good Man Speech. Piper knew it well.

"You've always been independent," her mother was saying, "but there's such a thing as being too stubborn. Before you know it, you'll wake up fifty, without anyone to share your life...."

Knowing from experience that it did no good to point out she was decades away from turning fifty, Piper stretched across the maroon-and-black-plaid couch. Might as well be comfy while she waited for her mother to wind down.

Though she'd escaped her small hometown of Rebecca, Texas, and now lived in Houston, Piper couldn't escape her family's shared belief that a woman's purpose in life was to get married. Piper's sole brush with matrimony had been a broken engagement that still left her with a sense of dazed relief—how had she come so close to spending her life with a man who'd wanted her to be someone different? When her sister, Daphne, had married, Piper thought the pressure would ease, that their mother would be happy to finally have a married daughter. Instead, Mrs. Jamieson was scandalized that her youngest was married, now pregnant, while her oldest didn't even date.

As her mom continued to wax ominous about the downfalls of growing old alone, Piper stared vacantly at the dead ficus tree in the corner of her living room. *I should water that poor thing.* Although, at this point, it was probably more in need of a dirge than H_2O.

"Piper! Are you even listening to me?"

"Y—mostly."

"I asked if that bagel man was still giving you trouble."

Mercifully, her mother had moved on to the next topic. Too bad Piper had no idea what that topic was. "Bagel?"

Then realization dawned. Her mother must mean Stanley Kagle, vice president of Callahan, Kagle and Munroe, the architectural firm where Piper worked as the only female draftsman. Make that drafts*woman*. In Kagle's unvoiced opinion, Piper's job description should be brewing coffee and answering phones with Ginger and Maria, the two secretaries who had been with the firm since it opened. Luckily, Callahan and Munroe held more liberated views.

"You mean Mr. Kagle, Mom?"

"Whichever one is always hassling you at work." She paused. "You know, you wouldn't have to work at all if you'd find a nice man and raise some babies."

Piper could actually *hear* her blood pressure rising. One of only a handful of female students in her degree program at Texas A&M, she'd busted her butt to excel in her drafting and detailing courses, and was now working even harder to prove herself amid her male colleagues. Why couldn't her family be proud of that? Proud of her?

"Mom, I like my job. I like my life. I wish you'd just accept that I'm happy."

"How happy could you be? Daphne says you're underappreciated and that one of your bosses has it in for you."

And thank you so much, Daphne, for passing on that information.

"Daph caught me after a rough week, and I was just venting," Piper said. "I love the actual drafting part." And loved the feeling she got when she was in the middle of a drawing and knew it was damn good, the pride of passing a building downtown and seeing one of *her* suspended walkways. If things continued to go well, Piper was hoping her next review with Callahan would lead to her first project as a team leader.

But better to argue her point in a language her mom could understand. "I'll admit to occasional work-related stress, but are you trying to tell me that marriage and motherhood are stress-free?"

Silence stretched across the phone line.

Aha! I have you there.

Then Mrs. Jamieson sighed as though this conversation epitomized her motherhood stress. "Honey, you aren't getting any younger, and women can't—"

Recognizing the introductory phrase of her Don't You Hear Your Biological Clock Ticking Speech, Piper interrupted. "I'd love to chat more Mom, but..." She thought fast, determined to rescue herself from this black hole of a conversation. "I have to run because I have dinner plans."

"You have a dinner date! With a *man?*"

Did she really want to lie to her mother? Piper gnawed at her lower lip. She'd already told one white lie. Besides, if it would save her from another round of "you'd be such a pretty girl if you just fixed yourself up," why not? Her imaginary person might as well be an imaginary man.

"Yes." Guilt over the uncharacteristic fib immediately niggled at her, but she pressed forward. "It's a man."

"Good heavens. I can't believe you let me go on all this time and didn't say anything about having a boyfriend!"

Boyfriend? She'd only meant to allude to a dinner date to buy herself some peace and quiet, not invent a full-blown relationship. "Wait, I—"

"What does your young man look like, dear?"

Piper blurted the first thing that came to mind. "Tall, dark and handsome." *Oh, very original!* "Dark-haired with green eyes," she elaborated.

"And you'll bring him home with you for the reunion, right?"

"Well, no, I—"

"We can't wait to meet him. I was hoping this weekend would give you the chance to get reacquainted with Charlie, but I didn't know you had a boyfriend."

"*Charlie?*" Piper would invent a dozen fake boyfriends before she let herself go down that road again. "Mom, I don't want to see Charlie."

Her mother's uneasy silence made it clear that it was too late for Piper to avoid her ex-fiancé.

"You've invited him for dinner or something, haven't you?" What did it take to convince people that she and Charlie were over? Not over in the-timing-just-wasn't-right, maybe-later kind of way. Over in the stone-cold, do-not-resuscitate, rest-in-peace kind of way.

"Piper, he's like one of the family."

More so than she was, it would seem.

"And I don't know why you sound so appalled whenever you mention him," her mother continued. "Charlie Conway is a good man, and he's the most eligible bachelor in the entire county."

That was probably true. Handsome, funny and smart, Charlie Conway had been a fellow Rebecca native and A&M student. He'd been so sought after in high school that Piper had been surprised when he pursued her in college. He'd claimed to love her because she was so refreshingly different from the girls they'd grown up with, and he'd eventually proposed. Their engagement had been strained, however, by his decision to return to Rebecca and carry on the Conway mayoral tradition, and Piper had returned the heirloom diamond ring when she realized that the allure of "refreshingly different" had faded. The longer she'd been with Charlie, the more he'd tried to change her.

"Mom, I don't care how eligible he is. He's not right for me." She'd tried to explain this before, but since she was rejecting the very lifestyle most of her family and childhood friends had chosen, they didn't quite understand. Piper knew they were fond of Charlie—she had been, too, at one point—but she hadn't liked the person she'd become when she was with him. "Promise me you're not going to spend the weekend trying to throw us together."

"Well, of course not, dear—not with this new young man in your life. We can't wait to meet him!" her mother repeated.

"I'll, um, see if he's available." Piper hated the blatant dishonesty, but not as much as she hated the thought of an entire weekend explaining why the county's most eligible bachelor wasn't good enough for her.

"This is so exciting," her mom said. "I can't wait to call everyone and let them know. Oh, and honey, if you're going out tonight, I hope you'll think about wearing a dress for a ch—"

Ding dong!

Piper jumped at the unexpected pealing of her doorbell. "Who—" Remembering that she was supposedly expecting a date, she swallowed the last of her question. "Gotta go now, see you this weekend. Love to Dad."

The doorbell shrilled again as she hung up, and a familiar male voice called through the door, "Piper? You home?"

Josh. Thank goodness, because a day like she'd had called for one of two things: venting to her best friend or a Chocomel, a chocolate-covered bar of caramel-and-nougat-filled nirvana. Talking to Josh was calorie-free.

"Hey," she greeted him as she opened the door. Joshua Weber was a co-worker who'd become her best friend after moving into her downtown Houston apartment building two years ago. "Did we have plans tonight and I forgot? I'm sorry, it's been a horrible day, and—"

"Relax, darlin'." His lips curved into the sexy smile that had no doubt been instrumental in seducing many women. Luckily for Piper, seduction wasn't high on her priority list. "We didn't have plans. I just wanted to see if you were interested in going with me for a bite to eat."

"What, no date tonight?"

Women flocked to Josh in droves. With his long lean build, square jaw, lionlike green-gold eyes and thick hair the color of rich chocolate, he was easily the best-looking man in the apartment complex. Maybe the zip code. Or the state.

"Dating can be exhausting." He leaned casually against the doorjamb, his posture matching his informal attire of a faded Astros shirt and jeans going threadbare at the knees. "Sometimes a guy just needs a little peace and quiet."

"So why not enjoy dinner alone in your apartment?" Piper asked.

It was what she'd planned to do. If she had any groceries. She'd been working so many late nights that she'd once again neglected shopping. Other women in her family were prizewinning cooks; Piper barely remembered to keep her fridge stocked.

"Being with you is even better," Josh said. "I don't have to be by myself, but I don't have to be 'on,' either. Besides," he added sheepishly, "I burned the nice dinner I was supposed to be having alone in my apartment right now."

She laughed. "Let me grab my purse and put my shoes back on." As she turned, she patted her French braid to make sure it was still presentable. A few strands fell around her face, but all in all, the braid had survived the day intact.

Good thing she hadn't yet changed from her tailored blue pantsuit into her comfy sweats. Josh probably wouldn't think anything of going out in public wearing a sweatsuit, but the casual look worked for him. For instance, Josh's hair always looked as though it had just outgrown that popular short and gelled style that was slightly spiky on top. Though it was still short, his hair was pleasantly rumpled with no trace of gel. Undeniably handsome when he dressed up for work or an occasionally formal date, he was somehow even more appealing in the rugged laid-back uniform of worn jeans and T-shirts.

The injustice of life. Piper in her oldest jeans was grunge personified, whereas Josh effortlessly resembled a female's fantasy come to life in any clothes. *Probably looks even more like a walking fantasy in no clothes at all.*

She blinked. Thoughts like that were trouble she didn't need, she reminded herself, sliding her feet into a pair of high-heeled navy slingbacks. The shoes were arguably the most feminine part of her wardrobe, but at barely five foot three, she'd take all the help she could get. Especially next to Josh's six foot one.

Grabbing her apartment keys off the coffee table, she stole a look at her tall, platonic friend. Emphasis on the platonic. She was perfectly happy without a guy in her life, and she'd watched Josh back away from enough relationships to know he didn't want a woman in his life. Not long-term, anyway.

And short-term's out of the question. Maybe hot flings with no future worked for some people, but the one impulsive time Piper had flung, she'd found the experience to be more embarrassing than pleasurable. She couldn't begin to fathom how awkward it would be if she constantly saw the flingee at the office.

Shoes on her feet, purse in her hand and lustful

thoughts relegated to the dark mental cellar where they belonged, she strolled back to where Josh was waiting. "All set."

Once they'd reached the apartment's parking garage, she turned to ask, "Who's driving?" But she didn't know why she bothered.

He'd already pulled out his keys and was striding toward his two-door sports car.

"It's just as well," she admitted. "I got another ticket today."

"Speeding again?" He shook his head. "I don't know how you manage to even get up *to* the speed limit with traffic as bad as it is, much less exceed it. Do the other cars just magically part for you?"

She climbed into the passenger side. "Hey, you're supposed to be sympathetic about my bad day."

"That's right. You said it was horrible." His low voice was full of teasing mischief as he turned the key in the ignition. "There are ways I could help take your mind off your troubles, sweetheart. You just say the word."

Piper's breath caught, a quiver of expectation in her abdomen. Josh's flirting was nothing new—it was his default mode—but tonight, after her earlier wayward thoughts, there was a split second where she forgot that he meant nothing by it.

Then he spoke again, his tone genuinely sympathetic. "Kagle being a chauvinistic creep?"

Although Stanley Kagle was too business-savvy to do or say anything overt she could formally complain about, his attitude was a constant reminder that she was the youngest and shortest on the drafting team. And the only one with ovaries, which he apparently viewed as some sort of handicap. Thank God for Callahan and Munroe to counter his presence, or she might actually have to brave the job market.

Piper sighed. "No, it's not one of our bosses making me crazy, it's one of our colleagues. If Smith doesn't get me those dimensions for the Fuqua building, my blueprints will be late, and you know who Kagle will blame. Then, of course, the traffic ticket on my way home today. And on top of everything, my mother called and..."

She'd been about to say that her mother was driving her nuts, but it seemed insensitive to complain. At least she had a mom. Josh's mother and father had both been killed in a car accident when he was very young. He didn't discuss his past much, but Piper knew it involved a lot of foster homes and very little stability.

"Grazzio's okay with you?" Josh's rhetorical question was an unnecessary formality. Even as he asked, he was steering his car into the parking lot of their favorite pizzeria.

They ate here an average of five times a month. On nice days, it was close enough to walk the few blocks between Grazzio's and their apartment complex, but on this rainy October night, she was glad for the warm shelter of the car. They hurried through the falling rain to the restaurant, where Josh held the door open for her.

Inside, the leggy brunette hostess greeted them by name, with a special smile for Josh. "Hey, handsome, when are we going out again?"

Josh winked at the woman he'd taken on a couple of dates back in August. "Ah, Nancy, I'd like nothing more than to sweep you off your feet here and now.

But you know George from the sports bar is crazy in love with you. I just can't break the poor guy's heart like that."

The hostess shook her head, laughing. "Well, if you change your mind about being noble, you have my number."

Piper thought Nancy would be wise to give up on Josh and give George, the bartender at Touchdown, a call. All over Houston, from the corner sports bar to the Astros' stadium, Piper and Josh ran into women who had briefly been part of his life and wanted to repeat the experience. Piper had been on the receiving end of more than a few envious glares from women, who, unlike Nancy, didn't know Piper had no interest in dating.

Her last relationship, the only one worth counting since Charlie, had ended when her boyfriend gently complained that her work was more of a priority than he was. She suspected that his intent had been for her to change that, but she'd encouraged him to find someone who would focus on him the way he deserved.

Piper and Josh were shown to an elevated booth with blue padded seats, and she stepped up to slide in across from him. An olive-skinned waiter with a mustache and faint accent took their drink orders and left them with a basket of warm bread. The buttery smell reminded her of her mother's kitchen, where something was always baking, and the upcoming weekend. Piper should be thinking of a way to get out of her impulsive lie, but the more she considered it, the more she liked the idea of a human buffer between her and Charlie. Piper knew from her sister that Charlie had most recently dated the town librarian, but he'd broken things off a few months ago, apparently deciding he wanted a more outspoken woman. Specifically Piper, the outspoken woman he hadn't valued enough when he'd been with her.

On her last birthday, he'd sent her jewelry that was too expensive to be justified by their growing up together. She'd returned the gift, but he'd still called her a few weeks later to let her know he was going to be in Houston. She'd told him truthfully that she was too busy trying to meet a project deadline to meet him for dinner and had hoped the reminder of her nontraditional priorities would dissuade him. If it hadn't, she could be in for a very long weekend.

Josh grabbed a roll. "I'm starving."

Lost in her own troubles, she barely heard him. She needed to be ready for her family, and she could think of only one way to do that. "Josh, I need a man."

2

PIPER'S DECLARATION was met with immediate choking on Josh's part. It wasn't often she had the satisfaction of catching him so off guard. Quite the contrary, he normally delighted in shocking her.

He recovered quickly, his grin suggestive. "Why didn't you say so back at your place? Forget the pizza, we—"

She laughed. "That's not what I was talking about."

Having decided that balancing the irritation of dating with her more important career wasn't worth the time and effort, Piper was pretty much living a life of celibacy. Josh's full knowledge of that was probably why he felt safe enough to flirt with her in the first place. No way would he ever actually go out with her. From what she'd observed, he liked to keep women at a certain distance, and he and Piper had passed that point already.

Though she admired plenty of things about Josh, his love life tended toward the...well, *shallow* seemed unkind, but the truth was some of his relationships made mud puddles look deep by comparison. Interestingly few of his dates complained, so Piper supposed it was none of her business. Josh didn't lecture her on her non-dating habits, and she didn't lecture him on the fact that he had the staying power of a— Actually, from the way ex-lovers swooned when they saw him, Piper suspected he had very impressive staying power.

She gulped down some water. "You know I'm going out of town for a few days, right?"

"Yeah. A family reunion." He smiled. "See? I listen."

"Well, I need a guy to go with me." She exhaled a gusty sigh that ruffled her bangs. "I sort of let my mother think I was dating someone, and she's expecting me to bring him home."

His expression turned blank, his mind obviously blown at trying to imagine Piper with a man in her life. "But you aren't seeing anyone."

"Thank you, Columbo. Nothing gets by you, does it?"

"Hey, watch the sarcasm," he said as the waiter returned. "You'll give me indigestion."

"Ready to order?" the waiter asked.

Piper and Josh exchanged guilty glances. Her "need a man" statement had distracted both of them from even opening their menus. As the waiter stood by, they debated what kind of pizza to get.

"We can split it," Josh proposed. "Get half of the pizza made one way and something different on the other half."

"No deal, Weber. Last time we did that, you tried the Jamaican chicken pizza, didn't like it and ate all of *my* half. Besides, I might just get pasta."

"Pasta?" Josh echoed. "Come on, this is the best pizzeria in Houston. You're going to come here and not get pizza? That makes as much sense as...you having a love life."

The impatient waiter clearing his throat stopped her from snapping a comeback.

"Perhaps I return in a few minutes?" the man offered.

Glancing from his menu to Piper, Josh said, "I know how much you like the Sicilian specialty. Want to just get that?"

Piper nodded, and the waiter shuffled off, appeased.

Josh immediately returned to the subject of her faux love life. "I don't get it. What made you lie to your mom? You never lie. Having witnessed you turn away persistent men at Touchdown, I would even say that you're sometimes *painfully* honest."

Lowering her gaze to the red-and-white checkered tablecloth, she mumbled, "I didn't set out to lie, exactly. I just exaggerated."

"Piper, when was the last time you had a date?"

"Okay, fine, I lied. I had to get off the phone! She called to remind me that I'm the unmarried shame of the family, and I cracked. I told her I had to run because I was meeting someone for dinner."

"And based on a supposed dinner date, she's now booking a church and auditioning caterers."

"For a guy who's never met my mother, you have a very clear understanding of her."

"You paint a vivid picture."

Piper bit her lower lip. "I have a real problem here."

"Nah, this isn't serious. A *problem* was Michelle. I can't believe she honestly expected me to remember her cat's birthday. And stalking me for two weeks like that after the breakup—"

"Maybe if you took the time to get to know some of these women before you went out with them, you'd pick up on little things like personality disorders." Piper hadn't meant to sound so snippy, but it annoyed her sometimes to watch Josh waste himself on a string of superficial relationships. Didn't he realize he had more to offer than that?

"Piper, people go out *in order* to get to know each other, and I'm not sure I want dating advice from a girl who hasn't been on one since the Nixon administration."

"Ha-ha. As if my family encouraged me to date as an infant." Though they probably would have if they'd known then how difficult it would be to marry her off.

"What I was saying," he continued, "is that I don't see why this is a serious problem. Let your mom think whatever she wants. Tell them he couldn't make it this weekend. Or that you broke up with the guy. Problem solved."

If only it were that easy. "I would, but Mom said it would really benefit Nana to see me with—" she groaned inwardly, "—'a good man.'"

His gaze locked with hers. "How is your grandmother?"

"Hanging in there, but...apparently not doing so well." She swallowed. "Last time we spoke, I argued with her. She was giving me more well-meaning advice on how to live my life, and I told her I was an adult and didn't need or want her interference. I shouldn't have said that."

Josh reached his hand across the table, and it hovered over hers. At the last minute he grabbed the bread basket as though that had been his intention all along.

She wasn't surprised that he shied away. Typical Josh. Weird that he dated and kissed and she-didn't-want-to-know-what-else with so many women, yet simple touches made him uncomfortable. Piper had grown up in a hug-oriented family herself, but she tried to respect the personal perimeter he maintained.

Though she had no trouble telling Josh about the familial reasons for needing a stand-in date, Piper didn't mention Charlie. Josh knew that she'd once dated Rebecca's current mayor, but Piper had downplayed the seriousness of the relationship. She was embarrassed that she, a modern independent woman, had been slowly altering everything from her work schedule to the way she wore her hair. It wasn't something she liked to think about, let alone discuss.

"So." Josh cleared his throat. "You're really going to take some guy home with you?"

"If I can find one," she said as the waiter approached. He set their pizza on the table, and Josh distributed the first cheesy slices. They ate in silence, mulling over her situation. At least, *she* was mulling. For all she knew, Josh was checking out a cute waitress.

To some, asking Josh to accompany her might seem an obvious answer. He'd certainly been willing to do her favors in the past—from free labor on her car to late-night assassinations of Texas-size spiders in her apartment. But this was different. While Josh came across as a people person who could shoot the breeze with anyone, he was intensely private. Piper had watched more than one woman lose him after pressuring him to "open up." A few days of Piper's meddling relatives interrogating him would doubtless be his idea of hell. Besides, how insensitive would she have to be to invite a man who'd never had a real family to a large family reunion?

So, with Josh out of the question, who was she going to ask? Instead of eating with her usual gusto, she nibbled her food, thinking out loud. "Most of the men I know are from work, and I can't ask any of them."

Josh nodded. "They might misconstrue the invitation, and you'd be in violation of the company's fraternization policy."

Plus she couldn't ask any of them for a huge favor when she wasn't exactly Ms. Popular at the office. She couldn't afford to chat in the break room when she was determined to prove herself, to get ahead in a field dominated by men. And she deliberately minimized any feminine assets, which some people had interpreted to mean she was aloof and hard. Though she and Josh had always gotten along professionally, they hadn't truly become friends until they'd run into each other in their building's laundry room.

"You know any nice guys?" she asked.

"I keep in touch with a few frat brothers from college, but I'm having trouble picturing you with anyone I once watched do a keg stand, then throw up on the front steps."

"What about that guy you coach softball with every spring? Adam?"

Josh worked with kids from underprivileged neighborhoods from March to June, and Piper had met Josh's co-coach during last year's district playoffs. Good-looking man, but she and Josh had agreed never to date each other's friends after an awkward situation when he'd broken up with one of Piper's former college classmates—another casualty of the Joshua Weber charm. Piper really pitied those women.

An unexpected thought struck her. Sure, she pitied them now, but how would she feel toward his dates if he ever showed a real attachment to one of them? Her stomach churned, but she told herself it was just the stress of her reunion predicament, nothing more.

"Adam would actually be a great choice for you to take to your parents," Josh agreed, "but he's in Vancouver on an extended business trip until after Halloween. Besides, what would I say? 'You remember my friend Piper—she needs a fake boyfriend.'"

"I have to find someone." She sat back, staring blankly across the table.

What would happen if she just told her family the truth—that she was single and liked it that way? *You know what would happen. Charlie.* The man had blond, all-American good looks and had been born into Rebecca's top social level. Granted, Rebecca wasn't big enough to have many levels, but the point was, he was used to getting his way. He'd seemed more bemused than upset when she'd broken their engagement, and she got the impression he was waiting for her to come to her senses.

Josh swallowed nervously. "Exactly why are you looking at me like that?"

Blinking, she chuckled at his wary tone. "Relax. I'm not asking you to come with me. I just needed a sympathetic ear."

He quickly replaced his guarded expression with a smile meant to be casual, but his relief was so palpable it was practically a third person in the booth. "Hey, here's an idea, what about a man from the gym? You're there every other morning. You've gotta know some guys."

"No, I spend most of my time with Gina. Or working out alone. I avoid eye contact with men so I don't end up trapped on the treadmill, fending off unoriginal lines like, 'Come here often?'"

"I can't help but notice you avoid men most everywhere you go."

"The last thing I expected from you is the Piper-needs-a-man speech." She drummed her fingers on the table. "I get it from plenty of other people."

"Sorry, I didn't mean to imply that. You definitely don't 'need' a guy. You're the most together woman I know." He flashed a wicked smile. "And I know lots of women."

She rolled her eyes.

"Give me something to work with," he prompted. "What did you tell your mom about this mystery man?"

"I told her he had dark hair—"

"Good. Thousands of guys must have dark hair."

"—and that he was tall—"

He laughed. "Compared to you, everyone's tall."

"—and I said he had green eyes." As the words left her mouth, she realized Josh had green eyes. Deep, forest-green with flecks of shimmering gold.

Not that she'd paid much attention.

Hating the sudden warmth in her cheeks, she blurted, "I think green naturally sprang to mind because my own eyes are green."

"Yours are blue."

"Blue-green." She ducked her head. "Close enough."

Okay, maybe she had subconsciously described a man who bore a slight, vague, infinitesimal resemblance to Josh. Made sense. He was the only guy she spent much time with.

It didn't mean anything. Yet her pulse refused to resume its normal rate. She almost pressed a hand over her rapidly beating heart, willing it to slow. After two years of observation, Piper knew that any woman foolish enough to let Josh affect her heart ended up with a broken one.

JOSH WALKED ACROSS the nondescript industrial carpet of the main workroom at Callahan, Kagle & Munroe, absently acknowledging greetings from a couple of draftsmen at their respective drawing stations. But his attention this Wednesday morning wasn't really on any of his co-workers—at least none of the male ones. He hadn't been able to focus his attention on work, either, which was why he'd decided to get a soda from the vending machine, motivated more by the chance to stretch his legs than by thirst.

As he approached the break room in the back, he glanced out the floor-to-ceiling window that boasted an impressive view of Houston's skyline. Of course, it would be even more impressive without the ubiquitous road crews and bright yellow machinery below and the gray blanket of smog overhead.

Not smog, just cloud cover. He hoped his cranky mood was due to this being the third consecutive day of autumn drizzle. Because the only other explanation for the irritability that had plagued him since seeing Piper home last night was her dating dilemma.

Her dilemma, he reminded himself. She'd said flat out that she wasn't asking him to go with her, thank God. After the last twenty years of being on his own, Josh wasn't sure he could stomach a weekend of parents and cousins, aunts and uncles all wanting to get to know the man in Piper's life.

Piper would figure out something. She was a determined, resourceful woman. Too bad she was gorgeous, as well. Her intelligence and sense of humor made her entirely too likable, and when combined with the incredible body she tried to hide under severe work attire and baggy weekend clothes—

Incredible body? He was not going there. Not now, not ever.

Except that lately, he had been. A lot. In the beginning of their unexpected friendship, her no-men oath and his own contrastingly busy love life had been a sufficient buffer, guaranteeing that neither of them would get any ideas about messing up their perfectly safe relationship. So what had changed? She still wasn't interested in romance in any form or fashion, and he still... Come to think of it, he *hadn't* been on as many dates lately. When had he slowed down?

He'd never intentionally set out to break Houston dating records, but it had only taken him a couple of breakups to realize he wasn't cut out for long-term relationships. The emotional distance that had helped protect him while being shuttled from one foster home to another didn't work well in romances, but the loner attitude that had been years in the making hadn't magically expired at age eighteen along with the state's wardship.

Though women might be attracted to him, more than one had decided he wasn't worth sticking around for; he was too used to keeping his own counsel, too guarded for "real intimacy." Maybe he'd been hurt once or twice when a woman walked out on him, but he wasn't complaining about the way his life had turned out. As long as he kept his relationships casual enough that no one heard wedding bells, he could have plenty of fun.

But that "fun" did not and would never include Piper. Their friendship had sort of crept up on him, originally built on a few chance meetings at their apartment complex, some venting about work and a shared affection for baseball and action movies. He wouldn't do anything to jeopardize their friendship—like hit on her.

Entering the break room, he reached for the spare change in his pants' pocket, but froze when he realized he wasn't alone. Clearly, the universe was testing him. Piper stood in the otherwise empty room, bent at the waist and peering into a cabinet below the sink. The short caramel-colored jacket she wore had risen above her hips, and the matching slacks hugged her curves in a taunting way that left him struggling not to look at her caramel-covered backside.

Poor choice of words. The color she was wearing didn't *really* resemble a sweet, sticky dessert topping, he told himself. It was more...well, hell. Women always seemed to have twelve words to describe one color, but he couldn't think of anything but caramel and the thick, sugary taste it left on his tongue.

He wasn't sure if he made a sound or if she'd just experienced that I'm-not-alone-anymore feeling, but she straightened suddenly, glancing over her shoulder.

"Josh! I didn't realize anyone was standing there. Hey, you don't happen to know where the extra coffee filters are, do you? I could have sworn they were in here."

"Uh...coffee filters? No. No idea." No alternate locations sprang to his hormone-impaired mind, but he needed something to distract her from resuming her under-the-sink search. Lord help him if she bent over again. "So, any new thoughts on how you're going to solve your problem?"

She leaned against the counter, her smile rueful. "You mean this weekend? Maybe. I think when I get home tonight, I'll call a few of the guys I've dated here in the city. I might not leave a relationship with *your* finesse and have them come back begging for more, but I think I'm still on speaking terms with everyone."

"Oh." Even though he knew Piper had dated, the thought of her with a guy jolted him. "Well, that's...great."

"If one of them actually says yes," she said. "I just hope it isn't Chase. I figure I might get desperate enough to ask him, but I won't be brokenhearted if he says no."

"Chase?" The only ex Josh remembered was Bobby. Or maybe it had been Rob. Definitely something in the Robert family.

"Yeah, Chase is one of those people with a strangely apt name. He spent the duration of our very brief relationship trying to get in my—" Suddenly, Piper's expression changed. If he didn't know her and her forthright nature better, he'd say she looked almost self-conscious. "Well, you know what I mean."

Josh's eyes met hers, and he hoped like hell his expression held no sign of the thoughts he'd been having so recently. "Yeah. I know."

Neither of them seemed to have anything to add then, so they stood without speaking, gazes still locked. Though probably not even a full minute passed, the silence stretched on too long to be entirely comfortable.

Piper looked away, glancing at the empty coffeepot on the counter. "I think I'm just gonna grab a soda and get back to work."

He pulled the forgotten change out of his pocket. "Me, too."

They both stepped toward the vending machine, then drew up short. Josh motioned with his hand, indicating that she should go first—mostly because it gave him a chance to regain his composure.

He was glad she was going away for the weekend. Maybe he'd just been spending too much time with her lately. Maybe his dry spell had boggled his thinking and was the logical explanation for the effect Piper was having on him. Sure, that was probably it. And once he found a date for this weekend, and Piper spent some time out of town, Josh would be fine.

He just wished his jaw didn't clench involuntarily every time he thought about Piper spending those days cuddled up to some faceless guy from her past.

3

PIPER WAS DOOMED.

After several fruitless phone calls and a long shower Wednesday evening, she was ready to concede defeat. As she'd rinsed shampoo from her hair, she'd mentally cast about for a last-minute possibility, but the truth was, she'd exhausted all her options. One ex hadn't remembered her, which had been a big ouch to the ego. Chase was busy this weekend, but seemed to think they should get together sometime soon and have sex. Robbie, her last hope and most amicable breakup, had happily informed her he was engaged. Apparently his fiancée would frown on the idea of his running away for the weekend with an old flame. Go figure.

I can't believe he's getting married next month. Has it really been that long since we split up?

Piper pulled on a pair of sweatpants, assuring herself that she didn't mind that her last date had been eons ago. She wasn't one for wasting time, and when you weren't actually looking for a relationship, dating was pointless. Why should she suffer through those pauses in conversation, those realizations that the person seated across from her was never really going to "get" her, when she'd rather be at home with her laptop and computer-assisted drafting software, getting ahead in her chosen career?

She supposed some people dated for companionship, but she had friends she could call on for company. Others might want dating for sex, but her experiences had left her convinced the whole thing was overrated. Pleasant, sure, but worth neither the awkwardness and risks of a casual affair nor the changes to her life to accommodate a relationship.

Maybe it was the guys she'd been with. Maybe a more experienced guy who knew women better, like, for instance, J—

"I do not need sex," she informed her empty apartment and dead ficus tree.

And she didn't need a man, either, she thought grumpily as she towel-dried her hair, then skimmed it back into a ponytail. Maybe she should just stick to her guns this weekend. Tell her family there'd been a misunderstanding—okay, a colossal deception—but that she was single and perfectly happy to stay that way. Of course, they were more likely to believe she was alone because she was pining for Charlie.

She strode across her living room and dug through her rolltop desk for the comfort of a Chocomel candy bar, but came up empty. A knock at her front door ended the sugar search. Given her current luck, it was probably the landlord with eviction papers. She considered her damp ponytail and heather-gray sweatsuit. Wouldn't win any fashion awards, but it covered all the necessary body parts.

When she opened the door, she found Josh, not the landlord. Josh's face was so grim that perhaps *he'd* just been evicted.

"I've been thinking, Piper."

Normally she would have made some joke at his expense, but his scowl discouraged it. "About?"

"You. Your situation, I mean."

He stepped inside, and she backed away with an alacrity she hoped he didn't notice. Earlier, when they'd been in the break room at work, she'd experienced a strange hypersensitivity to his nearness. Now, in the privacy of her apartment, it was magnified. Did he have any idea how good he smelled? A dizzying anticipation fluttered inside her, as if every part of her body was just waiting for the moment when his skin might accidentally touch hers. And she couldn't tell if she was nervous about it or looking forward to it.

Neither. Get a grip on yourself. She gestured toward the living room. It wasn't big, but the square footage there made it a lot safer than the small foyer. "Why don't you come in, have a seat?"

"Sure." He made his way to the plaid sofa. "Did you, uh, did you call any of the guys you used to date?"

Piper perched on the arm of the couch, pleased with the compromise between sitting with him and noticeably avoiding him. "Practically all of them, but then, my list wasn't that extensive."

"Any luck?"

"None whatsoever."

His posture sagged. For a second, his relaxed stance almost suggested *relief*, but then she realized his slumped shoulders must indicate disappointment for her.

He sucked in a jagged breath. "I've come to voluntarily enlist."

Josh wanted to go with her? She struggled to find her voice. "You're kidding."

"I might kid you about a lot of things, darlin', but this isn't one of them."

The familiar endearment stood out today, his warm, husky tone causing her stomach to turn a slow somersault. Her initial surprise and gratitude over his offer gave way to a momentary uncertainty about pretending to be romantically involved with him all weekend. The pretense would involve touching and—and...well, her mind was pretty much stuck on the touching. Her gaze slid involuntarily over his body.

"Unless you've come up with another solution?" he asked hopefully.

"Huh?" Piper blinked. "Oh. No. But are you sure? You sound like a man about to be martyred. You don't have to do this."

Which is why I offered, Josh thought. If she'd asked, he would have said no reflexively. Having no family of his own was almost tolerable as long as he wasn't around someone else's, reminded of everything lacking in his life. But she'd respected his space, reminding him again that she was the best friend he had. The reminder had relentlessly niggled at him, finally goading him into this decision.

His offer had nothing to do with the way he felt whenever he imagined some other man holding her or kissing her, whether the kisses were pretend or not.

"I never had a grandmother to take care of me," he heard himself say. "But you have one you love very much, and this would make her happy. Besides," he added with a smile, "I've never been one to turn down free food. What's a road trip between pals? I mean, it's not like anyone expects us to share a bedroom or anything."

She jumped up from where she'd been sitting, chuckling nervously. "Perish the thought. If we shared a room, Dad would pull out his Winchester and march you down to the courthouse, where your options would be marriage to me or the hanging tree."

"Hanging tree?"

"Sure, the big oak in the town square. They haven't used it in about a hundred years, but they'd happily make an exception for an outsider."

Josh peered up at her. "Gee, you make it sound like such a fun place, how could I not want to go?"

She caught her bottom lip between her teeth. He knew she'd never do that again if she realized it lured a man's gaze to her mouth, to her full bottom lip and the sweet curve of her upper lip. Piper didn't seek out men's attention. She wore her hair back, mostly skipped makeup and probably didn't even own a skirt, but her red-gold hair and turquoise eyes would attract a man even if she wore sackcloth. She applied the same determination at the gym as she did in all other areas of life, and the resulting figure would make any man's mouth water.

Any man's but mine.

With too few people in his life he cared about or trusted, Josh refused to throw away his friendship with Piper on sex. Not even hot and sweaty, mind-blowing, earth-shattering sex with the most delicious woman he'd ever seen. Which would never happen, anyway, because Piper would flatten him with one of her Tae-Bo moves if he ever suggested they hit the sheets.

When he sighed, Piper sat next to him, frowning. "You regret volunteering already."

"What? Oh, no. I was just...making a mental list of the stuff I should pack."

"What about work?" she asked doubtfully.

"I'll call in sick tomorrow and Friday. Don't feel guilty, I haven't taken a sick day all year and I'll lose them if I don't take them in the next two months." And it wasn't as though anyone from the office would guess he was with Piper. Though people knew they were friends, Josh's active dating life was common knowledge.

"You'll really do this?"

"You can count on me." Words that were as ironic as they were true. He'd never encouraged a woman to depend on him because the last thing he wanted was to lead one on. Why pretend he might stick around when goodbye was inevitable?

He'd been left too many times, and it was safer if *he* did the leaving, early enough that no one truly got hurt.

"I know I can count on you. Thanks, Josh." The poignant expression in her aquamarine gaze made him look away.

He stood. "If I'm going to pack, I should do laundry."

"Need any quarters?" She sounded uncharacteristically shy. "I did mine last night and still have some change."

"Nah, I'm good."

She rose then, hesitating briefly before throwing her arms around his shoulders. "Thank you."

Awkwardly, he returned the embrace, immediately recalling the last time she'd been this close to him. A few months ago, at a baseball game. They'd both jumped up, cheering as the Astros battled their way from a tie to a win. At the end of the game, Piper had turned to impulsively hug him.

The clean citrusy fragrance of her shampoo was exactly as he remembered. And the underlying womanly scent of her was the same, too.

He released her abruptly.

Piper shuffled back, her expression apologetic. "I just wanted you to know how much I appreciate this. I owe you."

"How about a lifetime supply of those chocolate chip pancakes you make?" He shrugged off her gratitude with a smile. "It's not that big a deal, really. How bad can one family reunion be?"

"You don't know my family."

"I'm not worried," he said. "And now you don't have to worry about this anymore. This weekend, I'm all yours."

SINCE ALL THE TREADMILLS were taken Thursday morning, Piper began a brisk lap around the indoor track surrounding the mirrored free-weight area. She supposed it was silly to be here so bright and early—okay, pitch-dark and early—on a vacation day, but she hadn't been able to sleep much after Josh's visit last night. Even after hours to get used to the idea, she was still surprised by his generosity.

On the surface, his favor might seem like a fairly simple thing. It was only a few days, after all, and a few harmless white lies to people who would never see him again. But Piper knew Josh better than that, realized what this would cost him. He'd heard her talk about her relatives enough to know what to expect—a convergence of people demanding to know his intentions and dragging out the details of the life story he hated discussing.

Knowing that she'd apparently underestimated him left her feeling both guilty and curious. If he *was* more capable of opening himself up to others than she'd given him credit for, was it possible that—

You're getting way ahead of yourself.

This was one weekend, nothing more. And Josh's relationship potential was none of her business, anyway, especially considering she didn't want a relationship. What she wanted was to prove to the people of her hometown that there was more than one type of success in life. Not having a ring on your finger or a significant other to fill your Friday nights didn't mean you were a failure.

As she finished her first quarter-mile, Piper spotted Gina Sanchez off to the side, stretching. A pretty woman with long black hair, a habitually wry smile and a collection of colorful T-shirts—including the one she currently wore that said Lawyers Do It Pro Bono—Gina was Piper's closest female friend. They frequently worked out together and sometimes caught a movie or dinner, but Piper generally turned down her friend's clubbing invitations to popular Houston hot spots.

Piper slowed her pace. "Morning."

"What are you doing here?" Gina stepped onto the track. "I thought you were leaving to go see your folks today."

"Not for another few hours."

Her friend shook her head, sending her dark ponytail swinging. "Ever heard of the concept of sleeping in?"

"Well, in the town I'll be visiting, the closest thing they have to a gym are the three machines in the high school weight room, only two of which ever work at the same time. And eating my mother's cooking for the next few days, I'm sure to come back ten pounds heavier. I figured one last workout would be good for me."

"You're so disciplined."

Piper raised her eyebrows. How was she any more disciplined than her friend, who attended the gym with the same regularity? "You're here most mornings at six, too."

"Yeah, but that's because I want to look good so I can find Mr. Right."

Piper just didn't get it. Her cousins she could maybe understand, since they'd been raised in such an old-fashioned setting where their peers aspired to good marriages shortly after high school. Gina's life was more contemporary than that. An attractive, self-reliant attorney, she nonetheless spent a lot of weekend nights with dates who didn't deserve her, only to agonize the following week over why they hadn't called and whether she would ever meet someone.

Piper knew that with her friend, it was more a case of *wanting* a relationship, not buying into the myth that women needed a man to take care of them. But honestly, why did Gina want something so much when it was usually a one-sided effort that left her grumbling about how there were no good men available?

Friends who'd known Piper post-Charlie had teased her, only half kiddingly, about her militant feminist streak. Maybe she *was* being too cynical, she thought as she pumped her arms in rhythm with her stride. After all, what was wrong with healthy equal partnerships?

Nothing, if they exist.

At first, Piper had thought that's what she had with Charlie, until his little manipulations had added up to one big picture. Never complaining that she preferred jeans to a more traditional feminine look, but buying her skirts for her birthday; insisting that children could wait while she built her career, yet managing to make sure she was holding some cute baby at every possible opportunity, hinting that she'd make a wonderful mother.

Charlie was just one example, true, but she didn't see a lot of counterexamples in the people around her. Gina's attempts to find a fulfilling partnership had yet to yield any convincing successes, and Piper's other closest friend, Josh, actively shunned emotional involvement.

Then there were Piper's relatives, the people she'd grown up watching. One could argue that her mother was happily married, but how happy could a woman really be while doing her husband's laundry and fixing his dinner and voting the way he voted? Personally, Piper would probably gnaw off her own arm to escape that kind of relationship. Her cousin Stella, divorced three times, obviously hadn't found the magic formula for true happiness, either.

Even Daphne, who in the past had echoed Piper's resolve not to end up like their mother, was now married and living in Rebecca, pregnant with twins. True, Daphne taught school instead of following their mom's homemaker path, but what had happened to Daphne's plans to travel and see the world? Her husband, Blaine, had apparently convinced her that staying in town so he could run his family's ranch was more important.

Frustration fueled Piper's gait, and neither she nor Gina spoke as they concentrated on their workout. It was only as they slowed to do one final cooldown lap that Piper caught her breath enough to relay the story of her mother's phone call and the resulting situation.

"You can imagine how shocked I was when Josh volunteered to go with me," she concluded.

Gina regarded her strangely. "Why is it shocking? You spend almost all your free time with the guy already. Is it even stretching the truth that much to hint you're a couple?"

Piper stopped so suddenly she almost tripped over her own sneakers. "Of course it is! You know our relationship is nothing like that."

Stepping off the track toward the free weights, Gina teased, "What I know is that you're close to a gorgeous straight man who has steady employment, yet you refuse to set me up with him."

Gina and Josh? They were all wrong for each other. They...they...actually, they were two attractive, intelligent people with a compatible sense of humor and similar career drives. Nonetheless, Piper had to restrain herself from snapping a warning that Josh was off-limits.

But she couldn't resist a quick reminder. "I've told you, we promised not to date each other's friends."

"From the way you make him sound and from the glimpses I've caught of him, I might be willing to ditch you as a friend." Gina grinned.

Piper halfheartedly returned the smile. Trying to atone for her inner snarkiness, she said, "It may not seem like it, but I'm doing you a favor not setting you up with him. Josh is a lot of fun, but he's hell on female hearts. You know how many women I've seen him break up with?"

"Maybe because he hasn't met the right one."

"Won't matter. Josh isn't going to let himself find the right one."

If the right woman dropped into his lap, he'd be too busy running the other way to notice. Not that Piper entirely blamed him for his behavior. With her close-knit—sometimes suffocatingly so—family, she didn't pretend to understand what it must have been like to grow up being bounced between foster homes. People coming and going through Josh's life as if it had some sort of invisible revolving door had probably become the norm for him. His dating habits now simply reflected the pattern.

"So this string of broken hearts, is that the reason you've never gone for him yourself?" Gina asked, surprisingly stubborn this morning. Normally all it took was one of Piper's we're-just-friends pronouncements to change the subject.

"I don't need a reason not to go for him. I'm not looking for romance, remember?"

Gina sighed. "And yet you're the one going away for the weekend with the sexy guy."

Yeah. Piper would love to laugh off her friend's comment—except the fact that she *was* going away for the weekend with a sexy guy was what had kept her awake all last night. How far would she and Josh need to go to convince others they were a couple? The man stiffened whenever she casually hugged him, and lately, she was no better. Yesterday, her entire body had tensed whenever he got close to her. So what would happen if he actually had to, say, kiss her?

And why didn't she believe her own self-assurances that she wasn't secretly dying to find out?

4

JOSH FOUND PIPER in the parking garage. She was loading the trunk of her car and glanced up with a smile when he called out a hello.

"Hi." She took his duffel from him, then unlocked the back door of the car to hang up his garment bag. Shutting the car door, she turned expectantly toward him. "Didn't you bring anything else?"

"Nope. I have everything I need."

"In a garment bag and one small duffel?"

Nodding, he peered through the car window at Piper's luggage. It appeared she'd packed the entire contents of her apartment. Maybe to avoid being robbed while she was out of town.

"I noticed the car was sagging," he kidded her, "but I thought we just needed to fill up the tires before we hit the freeway."

"I have presents to take home for the kids in the family, plus a gift for my sister, who's pregnant, another for my cousin who got engaged, one—"

His laugh cut her off. "It's your car. Bring as much as you want."

She slid in the driver's side and reached across to unlock his door.

Soon they were zooming down the road and Josh was clenching his fists in his lap. Usually, whenever he and Piper went somewhere, he drove or he took his car and met her there. Or he walked, or did whatever else was necessary to avoid riding with her when she was behind the wheel.

It wasn't just her tendency to drive at warp speed that bothered him; he detested being in situations where someone else was in control. He was a lousy passenger and he knew it. People disliked "backseat drivers," especially stubborn, independent people like Piper who hated to be told what to do.

I am going to keep my mouth shut, he told himself. As far as he knew, Piper had never had a single accident. She didn't need him to tell her how to drive.

His well-intended resolution lasted for about five minutes. Piper's head was nodding in time to the fast-paced song on the radio, her braid bobbing against the collar of her pale yellow shirt, and with each chorus, the car accelerated a little more.

"So," he blurted, "what's the speed limit on this road, anyway? We shot past the sign so fast I couldn't tell."

She glanced at the speedometer and immediately slowed the vehicle down.

He couldn't repress a sigh of relief. It was irrational to get nervous when he was in someone else's car, but for the first eighteen years of his life, he'd had no control whatsoever. He hated not being in charge of a situation. Usually, he managed to project an easygoing image, but his heart pounded every time he had to fly on a plane or ride with another driver.

For a while, his irrational feelings had even affected his job history, driving him to quit voluntarily before something beyond his power might force him to go. A few months ago, he'd started freelancing his services and it had started to pick up. He was regularly approached with jobs that were big enough to keep him busy, but too small for firms like C, K and M to expend energy on. Lately, he'd had to turn down as many assignments as he accepted, but he never backed too far away from his freelancing—and not because he needed the money. Life had taught him that little was permanent. Not jobs, not families, not lovers. Why get attached to people? Why give someone else the opportunity to leave him? He'd lost enough already.

First his parents, although he'd been so young that he remembered them mostly as faces in the photographs he owned. There'd been a string of foster families he'd stayed with only long enough to start caring before being yanked away and sent elsewhere. Living with the Wakefields had been the last time he'd really dared to hope for a family. After they'd moved, he'd decided becoming close to people was just an invitation to get hurt. He'd once dated a woman, Dana, who had tempted him to try to let someone in. He'd wanted to, he really had, but he'd never been able to adjust to the level of intimacy she'd needed. So she'd become just one more person to walk out of his life without looking back.

Piper zoomed beyond Houston's city limits, and for a moment he silently applauded her speed. Too bad he couldn't outrun the bitterness of his past with the same ease.

Maybe conversation would help alleviate his tension. "Is there anything in particular I should know about you?"

"What?" She sounded perplexed. "You know me pretty well already."

"Well, yeah, but is there something more personal, like you have a birthmark the shape of the state of Louisiana?"

"I do not have any weird birthmarks."

No doubt her skin was as creamy and flawless as her curves were intoxicating. "Okay, then some other obscure detail. Your favorite brand of bubble bath?"

"I'm more the hot shower type."

Her words erased the image he'd been conjuring up of thin, foamy bubbles barely covering her. But the shower comment only made him think of two people intertwined in a steamy tile stall—two very specific people who had no business being naked and wet together.

"Is there any reason you're trying to make me sound like a *Playboy* centerfold?" she challenged teasingly.

"Centerfold?" Cursing his exemplary visualization skills, he battled back an image of Piper scantily clad and provocatively posed.

"You know, those ridiculous interview bios." She adopted a higher-than-normal airheaded tone. "My name's Piper, and I enjoy champagne and bubble baths."

"Maybe my examples stunk. All I meant was, are there little things people might expect me to know about you? Things a lover would know?"

Her gaze shot from the road to Josh, and the word *lover* hung between them like an unfulfilled promise. Or a warning.

After a second, she shook her head. "Convincing my family we're involved is one thing, but trying to convince them we're having a scorching affair would be more complicated, not to mention a little creepy. These

are my *parents*, after all. Besides, people may think I'm
dating, but I never hinted that the relationship was serious. We just need to take small steps to make it look
real. You might have to, um, hold my hand or put your
arm around me or something."

"I can do that." Despite all the times he'd deliberately avoided those exact, seemingly simple, things.

"And..." She swallowed. "It might not hurt if they
see you kiss me once."

"Kiss you." Her summery citrus scent teased him,
and for the second time in as many days he wondered
what she'd taste like. Oranges? Sweet? Tangy?

"Just a quick peck or something," she said. "No
need for a major kiss."

Showed what she knew about him. If he was going
to do it, he would do it right.

"We got off track here," she said a bit breathlessly.

He'd have to take her word for it. His thoughts had
strayed so far afield that he didn't even remember the
original conversation.

"You were worried about personal trivia," she reminded him. "But no one's gonna quiz you about me.
They'll want to know all about *you*."

His least favorite topic. "Hope I don't disappoint
them. I'm not a very interesting guy."

She shot him such a knowing look, he added, "But if
there's anything you think you should know to make
this more believable, feel free to ask. I don't mind." He
ignored her snort of disbelief.

Relief pooled inside him when she didn't call his
bluff.

Instead, they lapsed into silence, the kind he would
feel obligated to fill with any other woman. But Piper

didn't expect him to be witty or charming. She didn't mind when he was obnoxious and cranky, and she could be obnoxious in return. Gradually relaxing, he leaned his seat back and closed his eyes, letting Piper's humming and the motion of the car lull his nerves.

He didn't wake up until he heard the sirens behind them.

PIPER'S GAZE FLEW to her rearview mirror, and her heart sank. Ignoring Josh's muffled laughter at her colorful language, she pulled the car over.

She'd been stopped twice in one week! "My insurance company is going to send a guy to break my kneecaps." She rolled down her window, looking up to meet the steel-gray eyes of a very tall patrolwoman.

With her platinum-blond hair and high supermodel cheekbones, the officer was probably a Nordic goddess when she smiled. At the moment, though, she was scowling. "License and proof of insurance, please. Do you know how fast you were going?"

Piper didn't think it would look very good if she admitted she had no idea. Before she could say anything at all, Josh leaned across her, addressing the officer.

"Afternoon, ma'am," he said, exaggerating his normal Texas drawl. "I just wanted to apologize. I'm the one who's got to be somewhere, and my sister was hurrying for me. I shouldn't have encouraged her to drive so fast." He flashed a full-voltage smile. "You should give me the ticket."

Piper mentally rolled her eyes. He was only going to irritate her. And what was he going to say when she asked where they had to be in such a hurry?

But the woman didn't ask. Instead, her cold gaze

turned smoky, and she smiled. "I don't think there's a need for anyone to get a ticket today. Your sister just needs to slow down."

Josh's voice was pure honey. "Thanks so much, Officer—?"

"Blake. Julie Blake."

"I suppose it would be too forward to ask if you're in the Houston phone book, Julie Blake?"

Unbelievable! The previously stone-faced officer actually *blushed.*

If they'd been in Josh's car instead of hers, Piper would have tossed her cookies right there on the dashboard.

After Officer Julie assured them she had a listed number, wished them a good day and sashayed back to her own vehicle, Piper let Josh have it. "What is wrong with you? Are you just one giant gland?"

"Hey, I appreciate the gratitude, but don't get all mushy or anything."

"Gratitude?" She forced herself to drive away slowly. "For what—the lesson in flirting? Thanks, but I've caught the Josh Weber seminar plenty of times."

"I wasn't fl— Okay, I was, but only to try and help save your kneecaps."

"What if your charm hadn't worked? What if you'd just made her mad?"

Josh stared at her. "Have you ever seen my charm fail?"

The question would have smacked of arrogance were it not for one thing: she never had seen his charm fail. Women adored him. Even she, who should know better, had been forced to admit lately that she wasn't completely impervious to his flirtations.

"I think you're jealous," he said, a smirk in his voice.

Exasperated, she almost threw her hands in the air, but decided not to, in the interests of steering. "Jealous? Of the Scandinavian patrolwoman?"

"I don't think 'Blake' is Scandinavian."

"I couldn't care less who you throw yourself at. You and Miss Swedish Cheekbones could—"

"I meant," Josh interjected, "jealous because I'm so much better with the opposite sex than you are. Face it, you're no expert on catching men."

"You make guys sound like fish. Or, more appropriately, a disease. For your information, and my mother's, my sister's and the entire population of Rebecca, Texas, I don't even want a man! So why would I work toward catching one?" *Gee, don't hold back, Piper.*

Though she'd surprised herself with her vehement response, Josh took her overreaction pretty well, simply shaking his head. "You know what? You're right, and I'm sorry."

She bit the inside of her lip. "Oh, great. Apologize and make it completely impossible for me to stay mad at you."

"I do my best. To tell you the truth, I don't even know why I'd say anything about you finding a guy when..."

"When what?"

"Nothing."

Piper risked glancing up from the road, but Josh's face gave nothing away. His eyes were shuttered, his mouth neither scowling nor even hinting at his usual flirtatious smile. In fact, it was almost eerie how expressionless his gaze was. Not vacant, but flat...as though he had no emotions at all.

Well, this trip was off to a fabulous start so far.

She pulled into the parking lot of a gas station. Silence reigned. Even if she'd known what to say, the very set of his shoulders deflected conversation. Not for the first time, she wondered what it must be like to love someone who could shut you out so completely with an instant, invisible wall.

But what must it be like for Josh, trapped on the other side of that wall?

Piper smiled at the ridiculous thought. He lived the life most bachelors dreamed of, and seemed perfectly content with it.

As she slid her credit card through the slot at the gas pump, Josh got out of the car. He crossed the parking lot, and Piper watched a group of college-age girls gape in open admiration. The man couldn't help his own appeal. She shouldn't have called him a giant gland when he was doing her a huge favor.

She was just a little on edge. This was her first trip home in years, and though she'd never admit it out loud, a herd of butterflies was stampeding in her stomach. The idea of pretending to be involved with Josh for the next few days was hardly steadying her nerves.

Still, she couldn't let him know the effect he had on her. Best case scenario, he'd tease her mercilessly until she had to kill him and hide his body on some deserted Texas road. Worst case, she'd make him uncomfortable and ruin their friendship.

She'd just finished filling the car when Josh appeared at her side, a brown paper bag in his hand.

"How about I drive for a while?" he offered. "And before you bite my head off, my offer has nothing to do with you going Mach 10. You know how antsy I get when other people are behind the wheel, and this way you don't have to do the whole trip yourself."

She surrendered her keys, knowing she probably shouldn't drive, anyway, when she was so preoccupied with her dubious homecoming. As she slid into the car and fastened her seat belt, he thrust the bag in her direction.

"I got these for you," he said. "I thought you might need them this weekend."

The paper crinkled as she unfolded the top and looked inside. Half-a-dozen Chocomels.

Piper grinned, the earlier tension between them gone. "You are the greatest, Joshua Weber." She savored the first bite of chocolate. "You know, I got to thinking about what you said earlier. You were wondering if we should know trivial facts about each other."

"Yeah, but you said they weren't important."

"They aren't. Not the trivial ones, anyway. But there are other things that might be. I hardly know anything about your childhood, and my family might think that's odd."

Okay, using her relatives as an excuse to pry was both flimsy and obvious. Luckily, Piper was curious enough not to be picky.

"You know where I grew up. You know I've lived in Texas all my life and went to the University of Texas on scholarship."

She folded her arms over her chest and waited, unwilling to be put off with vague answers.

He sighed. "How specific did you want me to be?"

"Maybe something a little more personal than the state you lived in."

"I didn't expect this from you," he said quietly, the very softness of his tone making her feel as though she'd betrayed him.

Perhaps she had. She'd known beforehand how he'd feel about this.

"Fair enough." She relented. "You don't want to talk, we don't have to. But my family's going to ask you questions this weekend. I'll support however you want to handle them, but you should probably give the matter some advance thought."

A few minutes of silence passed, and Piper turned to watch the flat autumn landscape roll by outside her window.

She almost jumped in her seat when Josh unexpectedly volunteered, "I lived in a total of six foster homes. The last family, the Wakefields, actually looked into adopting me. But they got transferred to Europe before the legal stuff could take place, so I stayed in an orphanage until college. A fraternity contact led me to a job in Houston, and you know the important stuff from there."

For a moment, she couldn't feel anything but surprise that he'd actually shared this with her, but then sympathy crowded out her first response. Six homes and none of them really his. "Josh, I—"

"It was great," he interrupted, his voice way too upbeat. "Like a cruise brochure. See new places, meet new people. Even got my own room once."

But never a family. Losing the Wakefields must've been like losing his parents all over again. "I'm so sor—"

"Don't." His gaze snapped toward her, and she saw the anger in his expression that belied his falsely cheerful tone. "My life turned out fine, and I wasn't looking for your pity. I wasn't looking to discuss this, period. But you're all so insistent."

You're all... Meaning women? Why had she pushed when she'd seen him withdraw time and time again from lovers who'd tried to force him into conversations he was uncomfortable having?

Maybe because you hoped you meant something different to him than those women.

The thought bothered her on many levels. Had she selfishly pried into a painful past just to prove something? And what was that "something," anyway? Josh was a friend, and they'd never be anything more. If she behaved so insensitively in the future, they might not even remain that.

"You misunderstood my apology," she said. "I'm not sorry for you, but for being nosy. It's none of my business. We all have parts of our lives we don't like to discuss, and I should've respected that."

He relaxed the set of his jaw, but his green-gold eyes sparked in a way that let her know she wasn't off the hook. "So what's the part *you* don't like to discuss?" he challenged.

She supposed she owed him this, and he should hear the whole story before this weekend, anyway. "Charlie Conway."

"Guy you dated in college, right?"

"Yeah." They'd had an instant bond on campus, being from the same hometown, but she'd still been surprised that he'd asked her out. In high school, he'd gone more for the school-spirit, cheerleader type. Piper, captain of the girl's softball team, had chosen shop over home ec. Not that she was the only one—

several other girls had decided shop was an excellent place to meet guys.

Piper took a deep breath. "Charlie and I were engaged for six months."

"What?" Josh's head jerked in her direction so quickly that she hoped for his sake Rebecca had a licensed chiropractor.

"He asked me to marry him. I said yes."

"You? You're the most anti-marriage woman I know."

She preferred to think of herself as anti-giving-up-your-identity-for-a-man. For years, she'd shaken her head as her father made the household decisions, swearing she would never be as passive as her mother or some of the other female role models Piper had had when she was younger. In eighth grade, she had felt personally let down when her favorite teacher married one of the junior high coaches and moved to a town where he'd been offered a job, even though the school didn't currently have an opening for her.

Piper wasn't unreasonable; she knew relationships meant making some concessions. Charlie had been her first lover, and she'd viewed their relationship with an excited idealism. The very fact that he'd lavishly praised her independence had made her want to prove she could compromise, too, to make little decisions that made him happy, like taking a class together that he was really enthusiastic about instead of the elective she didn't need but had found interesting. Over time, the issue of a three-hour-a-week art history class she hadn't taken somehow became the issue of how they should spend the rest of their lives.

After their engagement, he'd amended his plan to go

to law school and move to a big city, deciding instead he'd run as Rebecca's mayor. The decision itself had shaken her, but more upsetting was the fact that he hadn't discussed it with her at all. He'd simply made the resolution, figuring he could get her to agree to it later. It was sometime after that when she realized just how many things she had agreed to in the time they'd been together. He'd been molding her in small, subtle ways toward the very life she'd said from the start she didn't want.

Had her mother once been the same way? A free-spirited woman with her own goals, who'd sacrificed them one by one in the name of love and compromise? Only it wasn't compromise when just one person was giving in. As much as Piper loved her dad and her brother-in-law, sometimes she got really angry on behalf of her mother and sister. Then again, Mom and Daphne were adults, and Piper doubted they'd appreciate any interference. She just wished her family would afford her the same consideration.

"I can't believe you were engaged," Josh said, bringing her out of her thoughts. "Why did you wait until now to mention this?"

Why did he sound so accusing? "You're the one who was just saying we all had stuff we didn't like to discuss. Besides, you knew Charlie and I were together for a long time." She'd simply omitted the part about the ring and the short-lived search for wedding gowns.

Josh was quiet, and she wondered what he was thinking. She'd expected him to maybe tease her about her brush with matrimony, but he seemed almost angry.

Finally, he muttered, "I just can't believe you were engaged."

Looking back on it, neither could she. It had been a close call, but at least she could take comfort in knowing she'd learned from the mistake.

JOSH SQUINTED in the growing darkness to consult the directions Piper had written down. He'd been following the information on the piece of paper for over an hour now, since Piper had fallen asleep. If not for her deep, even breathing, he might have suspected she was feigning sleep to end what had become a tense conversation earlier.

Although, now that he thought about it, that type of avoidance was really more in line with *his* behavior than Piper's generally outspoken nature.

Of course, for an outspoken person, she'd been awfully secretive for the last two years on the subject of her engagement. He'd been so startled by her announcement he'd temporarily feared the car would end up in a ditch.

Before, she'd always made what happened with her and Charlie sound like a natural breakup, that they'd both wanted different things after college. The explanation had made sense, but what exactly had happened? And did she harbor unresolved issues that explained why she didn't date now? Was there a chance she actually missed the guy or wanted him back?

Oh, sure, she gave plenty of reasons for her lack of a love life, but Josh was still surprised that she didn't date. Piper might roll her eyes and call him a giant gland, but he'd noticed that she expressed her emotions physically. The hugs she impulsively doled out, the killer workouts she threw herself into when she was ticked about something—judging by them, the woman must be suppressing one hell of a sex drive.

You have no business contemplating her sex drive, he reminded himself. When he and Piper had first become friends, her disinterest in all things romance-and-relationship related had made her "safe." Knowing she didn't want anything beyond a platonic friendship had made her so easy to be with, he'd unintentionally let down his emotional guard. Maybe not enough to be comfortable discussing Dana or his past, but certainly more than he did with other women. Now, however, he regretted the diminished barrier between them, because lately, being alone with Piper seemed about as safe as being locked in a trunk with a swarm of killer bees.

And yet here you are with her this weekend, getting even more involved. Chump.

The sun had dipped over the horizon, but Josh could still make out the white mailbox with numbers matching the address Piper had written down. At the precise second he was realizing what a bad idea this weekend was, they'd arrived.

He slowed the car to turn right, passing over a metal cattle guard that jolted the car.

Piper yawned. "Wh-what is it? Are we lost?" She sounded almost hopeful.

"Nope. We're there. I think." He drove down a bumpy dirt road. "Is this supposed to be the drive-way?"

"More or less." She pulled down the visor and makeup mirror, checking her appearance and smoothing her braid. "You'll be able to see the house in a minute."

They crossed a small hill, and a white ranch house came into view. Josh steered the car onto the paved driveway and parked. A screen door clattered shut, and a group of people he couldn't quite get a look at in the darkness ambled down the steps of an old-fashioned wraparound front porch and into the yard, calling greetings.

Wearing the expression of a gladiator going to face the lions, Piper climbed out of the car. It was hard to say which one of them, she or Josh, was currently exhibiting less enthusiasm for the weekend that stretched ahead of them.

The first person to reach them was a man almost Josh's height, with blond hair and a wide smile. He bypassed Josh without so much as a curious glance and pulled Piper into a hug that lifted her off the ground.

"Piper! You're more beautiful than ever." The man kissed her cheek before setting her back down. "I've missed you."

The guy didn't seem to notice how strained her expression was, but Josh took a step toward her, sending what he hoped was a reassuring smile.

She returned the smile, though it didn't reach her eyes. "Josh, meet Charlie Conway."

5

JOSH DISLIKED Charlie Conway on sight.

Okay, maybe he had already begun disliking Conway before meeting him, but seeing the proprietary way the other man draped his arm across Piper's shoulders certainly didn't help matters.

Before Josh could politely—or not—remind Piper's ex that she'd dumped him ages ago, Charlie had hustled her farther up the yard, toward her parents. And away from Josh, who told himself the chill that rippled through him was due to the evening breeze, not the sense of once again being on the outside looking in.

A dark-haired woman who looked about thirteen months pregnant broke away from the cluster and approached him. "Don't worry, she hasn't thought twice about Charlie since the day she gave back the engagement ring."

Despite having his doubts about that, Josh smiled at the young woman. "I'm Josh. You must be Daphne Jamieson."

"Daphne Wallace, now." She indicated the bearded man who stepped up behind her. "This is my husband, Blaine."

Josh shook hands with each of them. "Nice to meet you both."

Blaine stared, making no attempt to hide the scrutiny in his brown eyes. "Same here. We've been anxious to meet you. Piper's never brought a guy home before—she must really be crazy about you."

Out of habit, Josh almost blurted, "We're just friends," but at the last moment remembered his role this weekend. "I'm crazy about her, too." His chest tightened as he said the words, and he told himself it was only because sentiment, even fake sentiment, made him uncomfortable.

Piper's mother descended on him just in time to hear his vow of affection, and she wrapped her arms around him in an enthusiastic hug. "I'm Astrid Jamieson."

"Nice to meet you, ma'am. Josh Weber." He had to wiggle away when she seemed reluctant to let go of him.

"Welcome to the family." Mrs. Jamieson winked. "Maybe there will be another wedding before too much longer."

"Mom!" Piper glared. "Try not to scare Josh off by prematurely planning our nuptials, okay?"

Mrs. Jamieson shot a knowing maternal look at her oldest daughter. "When you said you were *finally* seeing someone, I just knew it had to be Josh. The way you talk about him, Nana and I figured out months ago that you were in love with him. So what happened to get you to admit it at long last?"

Piper grabbed his hand. "Josh, I don't believe you've met my father. This is—"

He turned back to her mother. "Piper talks about me?"

"Oh, yes." Mrs. Jamieson was only too happy to answer. "She told me that you two work together, and that you're just brilliant at what you do. And that you're starting your own company!"

"Well," Josh began modestly, "I don't know if you can really call it a company yet, just some work I do on the side, but it turns a steady profit."

Piper's mother beamed. "Then you'll be a good provider. Such an important quality in a potential—"

"Mom! Don't say it."

"Husband." While all eyes were on her, Mrs. Jamieson added one last bit of praise. "Piper wasn't exaggerating when she said you were the best-looking man in Houston. She's been attracted to you from the moment you met."

"I never said that!"

Josh was sure she never had, but he was still surprised at her adamant protest. Didn't she want people to think they were attracted to one another?

Or—the thought struck like unexpected lightning from a clear sky—was her denial more for herself? Josh had never heard of *male* intuition before, but a small part of his mind suddenly seemed to flicker with insight. Even though he had no reason to believe Piper had been wrestling with the same desire he'd been fighting lately, he couldn't help but wonder if that was the case.

Or was he just projecting his own feelings of lust onto her?

Josh abandoned the mental debate as soon as he saw the way Charlie Conway was grinning at her denouncement.

The blond man sized her up as though she were a chocolate-fudge layer cake and he'd just discovered he had room left for dessert. "You mean you *aren't* attracted to him, Piper?"

Josh waited along with everyone else, wondering how she'd respond.

She quickly backpedaled. "Well, of course I am. I just don't think that's exactly what I said to Mom."

"My students would have said he's a hottie," her sister supplied. When her husband grunted, Daphne added, "I'm not blind."

Mrs. Jamieson continued her recitation for Josh. "She used to mention the constant stream of women you dated, and it was obvious to me that she was jealous of them. Took her long enough to admit her real feelings!"

Piper tugged on Josh's hand and forcibly dragged him away. "You still have to meet my father."

For her ears only, Josh whispered, "But I was so enjoying talking to your mom. This trip has been worth it already."

"Dad, this is Joshua Weber."

At least several inches taller than Josh and backlit by the light spilling from the house windows, Mr. Jamieson glared down at his daughter's suitor. "Son, I have a gun collection and no reservations about using it on you if you hurt my little girl."

"Really, Fred!" Mrs. Jamieson fisted her hands on her ample hips. "Maybe if you didn't scare all the young men off, she would've been married by now."

Daphne and Piper chided in unison, "Mom!" and Charlie cleared his throat, as though trying to remind everyone that *he* hadn't been scared off.

Fred Jamieson reached out to rumple Piper's bangs. "Don't you listen to her. Nothing wrong with taking your time and finding the right guy." He shot Josh an assessing glance, as though trying to determine if this would be the "right guy."

Charlie cleared his throat again. "I'm sure looking forward to one of Astrid's home-cooked meals. Who else is hungry?"

Amid murmurs of agreement, everyone shuffled toward the house. Josh hung back a little, smirking at Piper. "I didn't realize your family had heard so much about me." He was surprised at the warm glow that gave him inside.

Was it really so surprising that over the course of two years, she'd mentioned him to her family? After all, he'd certainly listened to her talk about her relatives plenty of times. But somehow he couldn't help grinning at the thought that he was a big enough part of Piper's life for the Jamiesons to have heard about his freelance endeavors and even his dating habits, although he hoped Piper had given them the G-rated version.

Reality intruded then, eliminating his foolish grin and reminding Josh that he didn't *want* to be a big part of someone's life. Nor did he want anyone to be a big part of his. That led to painful goodbyes.

Piper pressed a hand to her temple. "We've been here ten minutes and I'm ready to go home. This weekend is going to be a nightmare."

"Yeah, we should all have to live such nightmares, forced to spend time with family members who are excited to see us."

She did a double take at his tone, which if not flat-out angry was at least sarcastic as hell.

Where did that come from? He didn't blame her for her

surprise or her wounded expression. He'd always been a sounding board and a sympathetic ally, giving her no reason to suspect he'd turn on her like that. Truthfully, he understood why this weekend would be tough for her. Her mom seemed to allude to marriage every few minutes, and what was with the ex-fiancé's cameo appearance?

"Sorry, Piper, what I said didn't come out right."

"You sure about that?" She regarded him shrewdly, and he shifted his weight, feeling fidgety and once again regretting discussing his foster care past with her in the car, even if the conversation had been a short, vague one.

"I'm sure," he insisted. "I was just trying to find the silver lining for you. I mean, yes, parts of the weekend might be irritating, but on the plus side, they're thrilled to see you." Although Conway seemed a bit *too* thrilled.

The sound of Daphne's delicate "ahem" from the bottom porch step drifted through the night air. "Am I interrupting anything?"

"No," Piper and Josh chorused quickly.

His prompt denial stemmed from his relief at the opportunity to end the exchange. He suspected Piper's instant answer and nervous tone came from wondering if her complaints about her family members had been overheard by any of them.

Either way, their speedy "no's" sounded more like guilty yes's, and the porch light illuminated Daphne's face enough for her grin to be visible. "Well, I hate to break up whatever's going on out here, but Mom worries about the food getting cold. She wanted to know if you two would be long."

Josh seized the chance to escape. "I should go offer to help set the table or something, the least I can do to thank your mom for her trouble with dinner. If you'll excuse me, ladies."

He took the steps two at a time. Just as he was reaching for the screen door, he heard Piper ask, "What is Charlie doing here?"

That's what I'd like to know.

Daphne's voice floated through the darkness. "You guys go way back and we all grew up together. Is it so odd he'd like to catch up? Besides, Mom and Dad love having the mayor over to dinner. Makes them feel important. Enough about Charlie, though! Why didn't you call and tell me about you and Josh? I can't believe you'd keep something like this from me."

"It's not really serious, Daph."

"Oh, please...with the way you look at him?"

Even though he figured Daphne was only seeing what she expected to see, Josh still smiled over her words as he stepped inside the Jamiesons' foyer.

The hardwood floor was scuffed in a few places and the blue floral wallpaper was faded, but friendly voices and tantalizing aromas wafted from the kitchen. A real home. He swallowed the unwelcome lump of emotion lodged in his throat and started toward the voices, only to be practically knocked over by Piper, who was walking as fast as she normally drove. The screen door clattered shut behind her and her sister.

"I can't believe no one told me she was here!" Piper declared as she sped by.

A contrite Daphne followed. "I just assumed you knew."

Letting Piper hurry on ahead, Josh asked Daphne, "Everything okay?"

"Nana's inside, and Piper feels bad about not coming in to see her sooner. Nothing would have kept Nana from being here tonight, but the poor old dear just can't handle the nighttime chill."

"How is she?" Josh asked, knowing how worried Piper was about her grandmother.

Daphne wouldn't meet his gaze. "She has her good days and bad days."

They had reached the end of the hall and rounded the corner to the dining room. Though not elaborately decorated, the room possessed homey elegance. Simple lace curtains and a glass chandelier lent the room class, and a plain wooden china cabinet displayed plates and antique heirlooms that had undoubtedly been passed from one generation to the next. A rectangular table matching the cabinet dominated the Jamiesons' dining room.

His gaze moved to Piper, who knelt in front of her grandmother's chair.

She turned at the sound of his footsteps. "Josh, come meet my grandmother, Helen. Nana, this is—"

The white-haired woman lifted the spectacles she wore on a gold chain around her neck. "Step aside, girl. I want a look at him." She squinted her blue eyes and studied Josh so intently he half expected her to ask to see his teeth. Finally she lowered the spectacles. "Virile," she pronounced.

What kind of response was he supposed to make to that?

Nana solved his problem by speaking again before

he could. "I expect a man like you knows how to keep a woman happy?"

"I, er, try my best, ma'am."

"See that you do. My granddaughter deserves happiness." She held out her hand as imperiously as a queen, and he shook it, grinning.

Helen Jamieson was not what he'd expected. He'd envisioned a frail woman, covered by quilts. She was small and wizened with age, but her gaze was sharp and lively, as was her gamine smile. If he hadn't known otherwise, he would have guessed this woman hadn't been sick a day in her life.

Piper's mother informed them that dinner was ready, and Josh sat down with the rest of the family. The oak table groaned under the weight of steaming platters and casserole dishes. He was shocked when Mrs. Jamieson made two more trips to the kitchen, bringing out pans and baskets to line the sideboard.

Turning to Piper, Josh whispered, "Who else are we expecting for dinner?"

"Just us."

"You sure? Looks like your mom's feeding a company of Texas Rangers."

She smiled. "Welcome to the Jamiesons'. I hope you brought your appetite. And Josh...?" Though they'd been whispering already, her voice grew even softer as she leaned in closer. "Thank you."

He wanted to say it was no big deal. Hell, he wanted to say *anything,* but his thoughts collided in an indiscernible pileup when he realized how close her face was to his. Her sea-green eyes were wide, as though she'd just made some startling discovery. Her lips were parted gently, and his gaze slid to her mouth. She reacted immediately, her breath coming slightly faster, her cheeks blossoming with pale pink color.

The rosy blush made him wonder how warm her skin would be beneath his hands, but he was jarred from the pleasant contemplation by the sound of a chair being scraped across the wooden floor. Charlie had pulled back the seat on the other side of Piper, but before the man had a chance to plop down his mayoral posterior, Nana spoke up.

"Charlie, come and sit by me, won't you? I had some questions I wanted to ask you about city business, and my hearing isn't what it used to be."

Hesitating for only the briefest second, Charlie nodded. "Anything for you, Nana."

Piper's grandmother beamed a sweet, almost absentminded smile at him, but her eyes gleamed with what looked suspiciously like triumph.

The old gal didn't miss a trick, Josh thought. He couldn't help sharing some of Piper's fondness for the family's matriarch.

Astrid Jamieson began passing dishes around, and Josh's stomach rumbled in happy expectation of the chicken-fried steak, mashed potatoes and green beans with bacon. But by the time he was handed the basket of rolls, the salad bowl and the sweet potato casserole, he began to envision the button on his jeans shooting across the room and doing someone severe injury.

Piper's dad blessed the meal, and Josh dug in. After one bite of Mrs. Jamieson's home cooking, he resolved to somehow find room for all of it. It was the best food he'd tasted in his life. Definitely better than frozen pizzas that always turned out soggy in the middle, and microwaved bachelor meals that prompted him to date, just so he had a reason to frequent restaurants.

He smiled at Piper's mom. "Mrs. Jamieson, if the situation were different, I'd marry you."

Charlie raised his eyebrows. "I was under the impression that you weren't the marriage type. Didn't Astrid say something outside about 'a constant stream of women'? Sounds like you'd dated half the female population of Houston."

His jaw clenching at the other man's challenging tone, Josh said, "Probably closer to a quarter of the population. But the benefit of all that dating is that I can truly appreciate what I have in Piper, how special she is. Of course, I don't have to tell *you* that."

The mayor paused in the act of buttering a roll, his blue eyes as sharp and cold as icicles. "No, you don't. I know Piper quite well." The man put as much emphasis on *quite* as he no doubt thought he could get away with in front of her parents, but tempered the insinuation with an innocuous smile. "We grew up together and have such a history, you know."

"Yes, I understand you asked Piper to marry you. It certainly worked out well for me that she turned you down."

Charlie's face reddened, but before he could retort— or lunge across the table to disembowel Josh with the butter knife—Mrs. Jamieson jumped into the conversation, her hearty tone an obvious attempt to dispel the air of hostility that had gathered over the table like the electric atmosphere before a storm. "Glad you like the food," she said, responding to Josh's original comment. "I tried to teach both my girls to cook."

"Piper makes great chocolate chip pancakes," he said loyally.

Eyes narrowed, Charlie glanced from Josh to Piper and back again. "Eat breakfast together a lot, do you?"

Josh floundered for an answer that would shut his adversary up without sending Mr. Jamieson for the famed gun collection.

Piper rescued him. "It's one of the benefits of living in the same building. So, Mom, catch me up on all the local gossip."

Mrs. Jamieson launched into a recitation of what had happened to every citizen of Rebecca since Piper had left home, ending with, "Cousin Stella's latest divorce is final, and she just got back from San Antonio. She had her thighs vacuumed this time. And that nice Beth Ann Morrow you graduated with is pregnant." She glanced at Piper's flat stomach. "Beth Ann's mother is so lucky that she'll have grandchildren."

"Hey!" Daphne sounded as offended as Piper looked. "In a couple of months, you're going to have *two* of them."

Josh looked down the table at her. "You're having twins?"

"They run in Blaine's family," Daphne said with a nod.

Mr. Jamieson harrumphed. "When do you go on maternity leave? I don't like the idea of you working in this condition."

"I'm not fragile, Dad. I'm healthy as a horse. And about the same size as one. But I'm only working till the winter break. They hired someone else to take over next semester, and I'll have all summer at home with the babies before I go back. If I go back."

Next to Josh, Piper tensed in her chair. "*If* you go back?"

Daphne nodded. "Even with Mom's help and Blaine's mother...the twins'll be a handful, and they're only babies once."

"So you're thinking of leaving your students? Of becoming a *housewife?*"

Josh doubted Piper had any idea how shrill her tone was.

"Is there something wrong with being a housewife?" Mrs. Jamieson asked her oldest daughter pointedly.

"I love kids, myself." Charlie spoke up, despite the fact that no one had solicited his opinion on the matter. "How do you feel about children, Josh? See yourself as father material?"

Even though he'd expected this exact type of ambush, Josh faltered. He hadn't allowed himself to think of a real family in years, not since Dana and the realization that he just wasn't cut out for anything permanent. But now, the unbidden image of a child flashed through his mind...a child with aquamarine eyes that looked dangerously familiar. Josh's gaze swung to Piper, almost as though she were responsible for the mental picture and could make it go away.

Instead, his mind simply shifted to different, equally troubling territory. The way she was glaring across the table at Charlie shouldn't be a turn-on, but it was. Her turquoise eyes were brilliant, and her cheeks were stained with color. Josh couldn't help noticing the way her chest rose and fell with each angry breath, either. Did she even know how gorgeous she was, or how much he wanted her in unexpected, undisciplined moments like these?

Piper's laugh was forced. "Charlie, I thought it was Dad's job to interrogate the man in my life, not yours."

She stressed *the man in my life,* but in Josh's opinion, Charlie needed a stronger reminder that Piper was spoken for. At least, spoken for as far as everyone here knew.

Charlie's mouth fell open in a satisfyingly undignified expression, and he didn't seem to know how to respond.

Mr. Jamieson redirected the conversation. "So, Josh, you follow football?"

Josh was more of a baseball fan, but he contributed a remark here and there as Mr. Jamieson and Blaine discussed the Cowboys and the Texans. At least no one was debating a woman's proper role in society or making veiled innuendos about Piper belonging back with Charlie. Finally, the meal ended.

Mrs. Jamieson's attempts to talk everyone into second helpings were met with moans of protest. "Daphne? You're eating for three now. Piper, you could use a little filling out. Josh? More potatoes?"

Piper cut her eyes in Josh's direction and said sotto voce, "Think I'll clear the table before she starts her Young People Today Are Too Thin Speech."

"I'll help."

Charlie stood immediately. "I can lend a hand cleaning up, help show you where everything goes, Josh. This place is practically my second home."

He might as well have painted the word *outsider* on Josh's forehead in large red letters.

Bitternessburned Josh's tongue. When hadn't he

been the outsider? Although surrounded by a roomful of people, for one terrible second he felt completely alone.

As though she understood, Piper rose and touched his arm. The contact sparked through him, melting the sharp loneliness into something warm and full. And risky.

"Just help me get through this weekend," she murmured as they carried dishes to the kitchen, "and I promise you never have to come back."

She rinsed plates, and he stacked them in the dishwasher. Charlie carried dishes in from the adjoining dining room and found frequent excuses to reach between the two of them.

Annoyance simmered inside Josh. "I can't say I'm all that fond of your ex-boyfriend," he said in a low voice.

Piper's expression was bemused as she whispered, "Yeah, I think we all got that. I appreciate the jealous boyfriend act, but you don't have to put quite so much into it."

Though he knew it was irrational, he felt as though she were criticizing him, and thereby siding with Charlie. "If you want, I can drop the boyfriend act altogether...."

He trailed off as Charlie carried in a vegetable platter. The man just happened to brush against Piper before finally leaving the kitchen for more dishes.

Josh ground his teeth together. "As I was saying, if there's still something between the two of you that you want to explore, I can—"

"Are you kidding?" Her grimace, complete with eyes rounded in horror, did Josh's heart good. "That's not what I meant at all! As long as you're stuck here, I want you to be able to try to enjoy this weekend and not feel like you had to spend the whole time responding to his barbs, but he is one of the reasons I needed boyfriend camouflage. A big reason."

"Oh." Josh glanced at the doorway, noting that where he and Piper stood was visible to anyone in the dining room. "And your grandmother's fondest dream is to see you in the arms of a good man, right?" Even as he spoke, an internal voice cautioned, *Don't do it.*

"Right."

He took a step toward her and removed the bowl she was holding from her hand. Maybe he shouldn't do this, but how could just once hurt? Only to satisfy his curiosity and help him move on.

Bracing an arm on the counter behind her, he leaned forward, keeping his voice low. "I have an idea that should make your grandmother ecstatic." And Charlie considerably less so.

Piper's oceanic-colored eyes grew so wide he could drown in them. But her lashes fluttered, and her eyes closed as she stood on tiptoe to meet him. Then his lips were on hers.

Fire raced in his blood. As much as he'd tried not to, he had imagined holding her in his arms and kissing her just like this. Now, too late, he realized that the reality was far more devastating to his senses than the fantasy, and his assumption that he could walk away from "just one" kiss unaffected had been a foolish one.

Still, as long as he was making the mistake of kissing her, he should make the most of it.

6

SHOCK ZAPPED THROUGH Piper but was quickly replaced by a slow-throbbing desire. *Wait, this is not a good idea*, she tried to tell herself.

What else but desire could she feel when Josh nipped at her lower lip and teased the corner of her mouth with his tongue? She melted against him, parting her lips, and he deepened the kiss. There was no awkwardness, no bumping of noses, only wanting and a piercing sense of *rightness*.

Why hadn't they kissed like this months ago?

Some part of her seemed to recall that there were important answers to that question, but all she could focus on was the taste of him, the heat of his body against hers. Instead of satisfying any of the sensual hunger growing inside her, his addictive kiss only left her wanting more.

Her fingers went to the top of his shirt, to the button below his collar. She recalled his tight muscles and the sprinkling of dark hair she'd glimpsed a few times when they'd used the apartment pool. Boy, did she miss those summer months.... But she didn't just want to get his shirt off, she wanted—

"Heh-hm." From the dining room, Piper's father cleared his throat. Loudly.

She blinked at the reminder that there were witnesses, and slowly stepped away from Josh. Except that she couldn't get very far away, trapped as she was between him and the counter. A few more seconds of that potent kiss and she might have hopped up on the counter and invited Josh to end her self-imposed spell of celibacy.

What in the world had possessed her? Now that his mouth was no longer seducing hers, she could think more clearly. She wouldn't be doing anything with Josh on kitchen counters or anywhere else. Despite the liquid need pooling inside her and the sweet ache that had settled between her thighs.

"Piper, I—"

"We'll talk later." She averted her gaze, afraid of what she'd see in his eyes and what might still be visible in hers.

She harbored hope that they *wouldn't* discuss this later. What was there to say? He was only a friend. The kiss had been a pretense for her family, part of his favor to her this weekend.

Just because it had been the hottest kiss she'd experienced since...ever, that didn't mean anything. After all, he'd had lots of practice kissing women. Stood to reason he'd be good at it.

She focused on the dishes in the sink, determined to put the incident completely behind her.

Daphne maneuvered her way into the kitchen and set a couple of pans down. She nudged her sister and whispered, not quietly enough, in Piper's opinion, "Not that serious, huh? Looked pretty serious to me."

"It was only a kiss," Piper replied, irrationally riled by her sister's grin.

Daphne hooked one finger through the neckline of her daisy-print maternity dress and fanned the fabric back and forth. "Last time I saw a kiss that hot, it was in a movie." She winked at Josh, and he winked back, looking entirely too pleased with himself. Somehow the cheer the people around her were feeling made Piper's mood even darker.

She actually welcomed Charlie's scowl as he came through the doorway with a stack of plates, which he slammed down on the counter.

"Careful with those," Daphne chided. "They've been in the family forever."

Charlie apologized but still glowered, and Josh muttered, "My work here is done."

Aha! All the proof Piper needed that he'd only kissed her to help convince Charlie she wasn't interested in rekindling the old flame. But the confirmation left her feeling oddly hollow. Dissuading her ex, or any other eligible bachelors her family might try to foist on her, *was* one of the reasons she'd brought Josh with her. So why did she feel almost angry that it was the motivation behind Josh's kiss?

I am not angry. She scrubbed the plate in her hand so hard that the floral pattern almost came off with the food.

Okay, so what was she, then? Confused. Aroused. Curious. Had their shared kiss affected Josh as much as it had her? She could ask him later, but knew she wouldn't. What good would come from knowing that he'd been as turned on as she had? It wasn't as though either of them would ever act on their attraction, and if she'd ever needed evidence that men unnecessarily complicated things, she certainly had it now. She had a career to focus on, with an employer who would dismiss either her or Josh or both if they took the unlikely step of dating.

Of course, there was always the possibility that her worries were for nothing and the kiss *hadn't* shaken Josh as it had her. That prospect didn't make her feel any better.

Once the dishes were taken care of, and Josh and Piper had refused additional offers of dessert, Piper informed her family that it had been a long day and she wanted to go check into the hotel.

"So you and Josh are getting a room there?" Charlie asked. His petulant expression rendered him much less handsome.

"We're getting room*s*," Piper enunciated, "but that's really none of your business."

"I'm just trying to look out for an old friend."

Through gritted teeth, Piper repeated what she had been trying to tell her family for years. "I can look out for myself."

Her mother frowned. "But, dear, you have Josh for that now."

"Actually," Josh interjected, "Piper does great by herself. It's me who needs a keeper. She keeps me organized and focused."

Right then, Piper wanted to hug him more than ever. But it would probably be best if she didn't touch him again until her nerve endings stopped tingling from that kiss. Say, in forty or fifty years.

Everyone but Nana shuffled out onto the front porch and waved goodbye as Josh started the car.

"So," Piper began as he steered the vehicle down the driveway. "One night down. Think you can still stick it out the rest of the weekend, or do you feel a sudden emergency calling you back to Houston?"

His answering chuckle sounded weary. "I'll stick it out. I shudder to think what you'd do to me if I left you here to face them on your own. Although..."

"What?"

"Well, they do seem crazy about you."

She loved them, too, but it was easier from a few hundred miles away.

It wasn't just her mother's obsession with marriage that bothered her. Or her father's overprotectiveness, or even the occasional feeling that Daphne had defected. It was the hurt that came from feeling they weren't proud of her.

The only previous time she'd visited home after moving to Houston, she'd brought some rolled-up blueprints with her, wanting to show her family the work she did. Her mother never had made the time to sit down and look at the drawings, bustling off frequently to the kitchen to check on whatever was in the oven. Her dad had scanned the drawings, nodded once, then asked her if she was all set financially or needed him to write her a check. They seemed to have completely missed how important her career was to her, how determined she was to show that she could stand on her own two feet.

"Piper?" Josh interrupted her thoughts, for which she was grateful until she realized what he was saying. "About that kiss—"

"It was no big deal."

"No big deal?"

"Right." She wanted to dismiss the topic before he could point out the obvious, that he'd been doing it as part of their act. She knew darn well how he saw her—they were pals, chums, buddies, compadres. Until tonight, Josh had shown no sign of noticing she had two X chromosomes.

He flirted, of course, but that was just Josh being Josh. It had nothing to do with her. And thank heavens for that, because she certainly wouldn't want him to have any feelings for her. The buddy system was working just fine...or would be again as soon as her newly awakened hormones realized that tonight had been a false alarm, and returned to their dormant state.

Determined to downplay what had happened, she summed up the subject before he could. "Suffice it to say, I appreciate the favor. It wasn't too bad, and we might even have to do it again, but only in front of the necessary witnesses, of course."

"Of course." He bit out the words, and she wondered if she should have expressed more gratitude for the way he'd helped her.

Long moments later, as they drove down the dark country road, he spoke again, sounding like his normal self. "I don't mean to disparage your hometown, Piper, but it's creepy out here."

She tore her gaze away from the millions of stars she could see out her window and shot him a questioning glance. "Creepy? I can't believe a man who braves Houston's crime rate would get spooked out here."

"We've been on the road ten minutes and haven't seen a single car. I find that disconcerting."

"Most people around here go to bed by nine."

"Sounds like a fascinating place to live."

"Maybe it's not the most exciting town, but it's clean and friendly and—" It was probably the first time she'd said something nice about her hometown since she'd left. "Anyway, it's not too bad. It's just not for me, and one of the main reasons Charlie and I broke up."

"When you say 'broke up,' just how mutual was that?"

"Not at all, as you probably guessed by tonight. It was my decision." She stopped there, not wanting to get into a Charlie-bashing session, despite how pompous the man had been this evening.

How could it be fair to catalog Charlie's faults in front of Josh? Charlie had followed in the well-worn path of generations of Rebecca mayors before him, not because he'd ever said convincingly that it was what he wanted, but because it was easier than doing something different. She couldn't imagine Charlie ever striking out on his own or taking initiative the way Josh did with his sideline business, which he ran on the weekends. Besides, even though Charlie was regarded as the catch of the town, she couldn't picture anyone preferring the blond, bland mayor to her wickedly handsome best friend and his lethal kisses. Telling a man with Josh's charisma about Charlie's shortcomings seemed as sporting as letting Sammy Sosa come to bat against a Little League team.

So Piper opted to change the subject and give Josh directions instead. He turned the car to the left, and the hotel's blue neon sign appeared up ahead.

"Did you deliberately pick a place this far from your parents?" he asked.

She laughed. "Options are a little more limited out here than in Houston. There are only two real hotels in the whole county, and this one's the best. It won't be the Waldorf, but rates are reasonable and it should be clean."

"Hey, I'm not picky about our digs. I'm just surprised your family didn't insist we stay with them."

"They would have, but I didn't commit to coming for the reunion until my aunt and uncle from Louisiana had already arranged to stay with my parents. They'll get in tomorrow."

As Josh parked the car in front of the hotel, Piper suddenly realized how tired she was. She'd been so tense about coming home that she'd let anxiety wear her down, and she hadn't had a decent night's sleep since she'd first told her mother about her "boyfriend." Now, with the hardest part of the weekend—the first contact—behind her, exhaustion replaced the anticipatory stress.

While they checked in at the front desk, Piper yawned repeatedly, struggling to focus her eyes on the paperwork in front of her. The trek up the staircase to their reserved rooms seemed as grueling as a workout on the StairMaster. She couldn't remember ever being as happy to see anything as the door with her room number on it. Mumbling a good-night to Josh, she shuffled inside, hoping she could make it as far as the bed. She toyed with the idea of not brushing her teeth and just sleeping in what she was wearing.

A sudden knock startled her into dropping a suitcase on her foot. Muttering "ouch" and other words of the four-letter variety, she hobbled toward the door to the hallway, then realized that wasn't where the knock had originated.

For the first time, she noticed another door, next to

the bed. She opened it hesitantly and found Josh smiling at her.

Over his jeans, he wore a shirt that was now half-unbuttoned. Her fingers itched to finish the job for him.

"I forgot to pack toothpaste," he said.

"There's a door between our rooms?"

He didn't bother answering the obvious. "So do you have toothpaste I can borrow in one of those hundreds of bags you brought?"

She kept staring. Under her gaze, he slipped the last few buttons out of their holes and shrugged off his shirt and pitched it into the room behind him. She didn't blame him—damn, it was getting warm in here. She couldn't tell from his facial expression if he was matter-of-factly getting ready for bed or if he was teasing her. Of course, it would be easier to gauge his expression if she actually looked up at his *face*. As it was, she couldn't lift her gaze from the taut planes of his chest. Instead, her eyes trailed downward, following the fine line of hair that bisected his sculpted abs, leading past his navel to the fly of his jeans.

Realizing where she was staring, she jerked her head up to find him watching her. The good news was he wasn't laughing at her. The bad news was enough speculative heat danced in his eyes to warm the entire hotel.

"About that toothpaste?" he prompted. "You never know when minty fresh breath will come in handy."

"Uh, sure...if you want to just go back into your room and finish getting dressed for bed, I can bring you the toothpaste in a minute." Maybe that would buy her time to get her suddenly cardboard tongue unstuck from the roof of her inexplicably dry mouth.

"I don't actually get dressed for bed, Piper. Just *un*-dressed." He flashed a wicked smile. "I could go ahead and do that, but—"

"No! No, that's okay. I didn't realize that you slept n— I mean, I didn't... Just have a seat and give me a sec, will ya?" Maybe if she tried really hard, she could embarrass herself further. Go for some kind of record.

If she'd been more awake at the beginning of this unexpected encounter, she would have handled it more gracefully. At least, that was the story she was sticking to. He sat on the edge of her bed, waiting while she rummaged through her duffel bag. Why couldn't he have used the chair on the other side of the room, next to the window?

So what if he's in my room, on my bed? It's only Josh.
Only? Ha!

She knew instinctively that she wouldn't be reacting to any other man this way. But it seemed something about Josh—lately, *everything* about Josh—made her go as warm and gooey as a Chocomel left to melt in a car on a sunny day.

A strange thrumming sound rang in Piper's ears. Probably her hormones chanting their demands. Well, as she'd explained to Josh before, she had total control over her hormones. She wasn't going to allow some chemical reaction in her body to rule her actions.

Exhaustion and her conflicting emotions impaired her thinking. Then, of course, there was the distraction of the sexiest man she'd ever seen currently lounging on her bedspread—not that she'd need the blanket to keep her warm if he stayed.

She blinked. He was not staying.

"Here." She thrust the tube of toothpaste at him. "Take it. Give it back to me in the morning."

"You want to use some first?"

"I'll skip it tonight, I'm so beat. You just be on your way, and I'll crawl into bed."

He paused in the doorway, where she waited to close the door. His gaze seduced hers, so warm and compelling she couldn't look away. Moving slowly, almost hypnotically, he inclined his head toward her. Her heart beat so loudly she was afraid he must hear it. The people in the room below could probably hear it.

He wasn't going to kiss her, was he? She'd made a point of mentioning earlier that they only needed to keep up the pretense in front of witnesses.

Maybe you need to practice so that it looks natural in front of your family, a small voice rationalized.

But he obviously wasn't listening to a similar small voice. At the last minute, he stopped short and whispered, "Good night, Piper," before backing into the dim shadows of his own room.

She shut the door, replaying the last few seconds in her head, wondering where she'd gone wrong. *Good night, Piper?* She'd been so sure that... *You didn't want him to kiss you, remember?*

Right. It was probably best that he hadn't. Why complicate things further? Besides, despite her attempted rationalization, she knew from their earlier experience in her parents' kitchen that Josh needed no practice. You couldn't improve on sensual perfection.

Time to forget about all that, she told herself. He was gone now, and she was finally free to pull on a long T-shirt and crawl between the clean cool sheets to fall into a restful sleep.

As if that was going to happen. The hotel mattress bore the imprint of Josh's body, and with the subtle spice of his cologne still lacing the space around her, it was easy to imagine him here. With her.

Piper kicked off the sheets, needing air against her flushed and fevered skin. She reminded herself that a love life was almost never worth the time and energy it required. But one with Josh? Okay, so that might definitely be worth something, but not her entire career. She'd worked hard to position herself at C, K and M, and was hopeful that she'd be assigned some big projects after her next review. The last thing she wanted to do was start over elsewhere—especially for a brief fling.

Now if it were for a full-blown relationship... No. She didn't want one of those, either. They were like quicksand. What if she slipped into one and slowly lost her identity before she realized it? What if one day in the future she woke up like Daphne, who also had had plans for her life? What if Piper were the one sitting at the dining room table, announcing to her family that she'd decided to give up her goals and occupation? After all, she'd almost headed down that road with Charlie, and she didn't remember him ever having the magnetic pull on her that she'd experienced moments ago with Josh.

She was just tired. It had been a long day, and this would all look a lot clearer in the morning, after some sleep.

But how was she supposed to sleep when the only thing between her and Josh's naked body was one lousy door so thin she could hear him stretch across his own bed on the other side?

"REMIND ME WHAT the agenda for this morning is," Josh said as she pulled the car up to the ranch house.

She was guiltily grateful he hadn't asked about the whole day. She hadn't yet figured out how to pass on what her mom had told her last night. Piper had meant to explain about the shower, but that kiss had short-circuited her brain.

"I have to do girl stuff," Piper said, "and you'll—"

"Let me guess. Guy stuff?"

She rolled her eyes. "I figured you could hang out with Dad. Unless you want to go with me to see my cousin's wedding dress and then take Daphne to the OB."

"I'll take my chances with your dad."

"Good choice. Don't worry, it'll be fun. Now, if Dad asks what attracted you to me, make sure you pick an answer that isn't physical." She switched off the ignition. "I mean, don't get too carried away with the whole boyfriend pretense. I'm not saying you're actually turned on by me."

As they climbed out of the car, Josh laughed. "That sounded like a question. Are you fishing, Piper?"

"What? No, of course not." If her slightly raised voice sounded defensive, that was a coincidence.

"Uh-oh. Sounds like a fight." Charlie's unexpected voice came from the porch. "I certainly hope there isn't trouble in paradise."

"As I recall," Josh muttered, "the only trouble in paradise was an uninvited snake trying to cause problems."

Ignoring him, Piper glanced at Charlie, wondering just how persistent he'd be this weekend. She'd expected him to take the hint last night. She managed a smile, but her tone was pointed. "What brings you here this morning?"

Charlie shrugged. "I told your dad I'd come out early and help him load bales of hay to take to your uncle."

"Well, that was...nice."

Behind her, Josh made a small noise.

"It eases my conscience a bit for the way I behaved with you. It sounds trite, but I really didn't know what I had until it...until *you* were gone." Charlie continued as if Josh weren't even with her. "It wasn't all bad, though, right? We had some good times, Piper."

They had, but the last thing she wanted to do was encourage him to dwell on them.

"Some, but that's all in the past. The distant past." Besides, she suspected his continued pursuit was fueled as much by the novelty of his not being able to have her as it was by fond memories. "I'm with Josh now."

To reinforce her words, Josh loyally stepped up behind her, aligning his body against hers and draping his arm around her waist, across the top of her black jeans. A dizzy sensation accompanied his nearness. Piper blinked, but then closed her eyes completely when Josh pushed aside her ponytail and brushed a soft kiss to the back of her vulnerable neck. His lips were feather-light on her skin, so how did they wring such a potent response?

The front door banged shut, startling her. She took a step forward, deciding that regaining her sanity was more important than fooling her family at the moment. Daphne made her way down the porch steps, glaring daggers at Charlie. Then she turned to her sister with an apologetic sorry-he-got-away-from-me expression.

Piper smiled. "You ready to go, Daph?"

"Yeah. I appreciate your giving me a ride to the doctor. Blaine didn't want to take off work this morning since he's leaving early this afternoon, and today's Mom's day for helping out at Nana's retirement center. Mornin', Josh. What are your plans?"

"Hanging out with your dad. Piper said it would be fun."

"Uh-huh." Daphne's eyebrows shot up. "If that's what she said."

"Don't worry." Charlie insinuated himself into the conversation. "I'll be here, too. And I can certainly help put Josh at ease."

Piper bit back a sarcastic retort and shot Josh a look asking that he do the same. Open antagonism hadn't accomplished anything, so she was hoping that maybe an if-we-ignore-him-he'll-go-away strategy would have better results.

Daphne offered a weak wave to the guys. "Have a good day. Josh, I'll see you this afternoon at the—" She broke off sheepishly, with a sidelong glance at Charlie. "The, um, thing."

"What thing?" both men asked on cue.

Damn. Piper still hadn't explained about the shower. Well, now was a good time, what with the getaway car so close. She caught Josh's eye and motioned him aside. They walked across the grass toward her parents' barn. "Do you remember me mentioning that my family used the reunion weekend to celebrate a bunch of things at once?"

"Sure." He shoved his hands into the pockets of his khaki slacks.

"Well, the actual reunion is tomorrow, but this afternoon, some local family members and friends of Daphne and Mandy are getting together."

"Should I know who Mandy is?"

"My cousin," she reminded him. "The engaged one, whose wedding dress Daphne and I are going to see. Which leads me back to this afternoon... It's a combination baby shower for my sister and bridal shower for my cousin. A couples shower, and you're my date." She took a breath, praying he wouldn't go nuclear on her.

"I have to go to a baby shower *and* a bridal shower? Any chance you're just kidding to get back at me for past short jokes?"

"Actually, the fact that I'm *not* kidding is my way of getting back at you."

He looked unamused.

"I knew there would be a shower this weekend, but I assumed it was ladies only," she said. "When Mom told me last night it was a couples shower...I should've mentioned it, I know." She'd truly meant to, but she'd become preoccupied with other matters, like not using that door between their rooms to sneak into his bed and fulfill those fantasies she'd had all night.

"Piper, I'm a guy. A guy who watches sports on ESPN from my recliner. I don't sit around baby showers and—I don't even know what it is you sit around doing at baby showers."

"I'll make you chocolate chip pancakes for a year."

He was shaking his head before she even finished voicing the offer. "This is bigger than pancakes." He scowled as though bamboo shoots shoved under his fingernails would be less painful than spending a few hours watching a bride and mother-to-be open some presents.

Piper empathized with his pain. A very small part of her, one she wasn't proud of, was even glad he'd be there suffering alongside her. Probably best not to let him know about that part.

She sent a quick, worried glance toward Daphne and Charlie, who were having their own tense discussion. "Please, Josh? It'll just be one afternoon."

"All right, I'll go." He ran a hand through his dark hair. "But you owe me."

"Anything you want," she agreed automatically.

7

"ANYTHING I WANT? Well, in that case..." Josh's eyes darkened, the golden glints shimmering with new mischief. "I'm sure that by this afternoon, I'll have a list. I don't suppose any place around here sells flavored body lotion?"

He's only joking, Piper told herself. Josh was teasing her, flirting as always. But it didn't feel that way. The heat she might have expected to be burning in her face was joined by liquid warmth pooling in lower, more intimate places. Since when did she respond to him like that?

But over the last few days, it had become difficult to recall a time she *hadn't* responded this way. He met her eyes then, and his playful smile faded into something more serious, more dangerous than his outrageous teasing had ever been.

Trying to sound amused, she managed a choked laugh. "Flavored body lotion? In Rebecca? Please. You have to drive to the next county just to find a grocery store that sells beer."

"Just as well," he said. "After tasting your kiss last night, I can't imagine there's any part of you that would be enhanced by artificial flavoring."

"*Josh!*" She'd meant the name to be a warning to stave off further outrageousness, instead she sounded like a woman issuing an invitation. An invitation he intended to take her up on, judging by the way he angled his head toward her.

Her breath mingled with his, but before their lips actually made contact, Daphne called out, "Hey, Piper, I don't mean to interrupt you, but—"

Piper had never been so glad to be interrupted in all her life. "Be right there!" She practically hurled herself in the direction of the car, but she could feel Josh's gaze on her as she retreated. And even the engine coming to life as she turned the ignition didn't drown the echo of his soft, knowing chuckle in her ears.

As Piper drove to the local bridal boutique, Daphne asked if everything was okay.

"Fine." With the possible exception of a pulse so rapid and a body temperature so high that Piper should probably have skipped her cousin's wedding dress fitting and driven straight to the ER.

"You're awfully quiet," Daphne observed. "Did I interrupt an important moment between you and Josh?"

Recalling that moment, Piper found it was all she could do not to melt into a puddle in the driver's seat. "I was just filling him in on the details of the shower."

"About that," Daphne said. "Charlie's going to be there, too."

"He's coming to a couples shower? With whom?"

"By himself, I'm afraid. He wasn't on the original guest list, despite Mom's urging, but when I accidentally mentioned the shower... What was I supposed to do? He knew Josh was going, and I've known Josh for about twelve hours. I've known Charlie Conway all my life."

Piper sighed. Daphne looked repentant already, and besides, she was right.

"The more the merrier," Piper replied.

Her sister changed the subject. "You sure you want to risk your relationship with Josh by leaving him with Dad all morning?"

"Josh is tough." Plus, she might have been more worried if there was an actual relationship to risk. "He won't break."

"Don't you remember what Dad did when Blaine and I were dating? He said they should spend the day together and discuss Blaine's intentions, man to man. He took Blaine riding and put him on Thunder, for heaven's sake. Poor Blaine was so sore that, for a while, we didn't think he'd be able to father children."

Piper slanted her gaze toward her sister's stomach, which almost reached the dashboard even though the seat was pushed back as far as it could go. "I'd say that worry was for nothing. Besides, wasn't Thunder Dad's paternal retaliation at finding the two of you making out in the barn?"

"And you don't think he saw you and Josh in the kitchen last night?"

Piper's face warmed. "That was just a kiss."

"So you said."

"Why do you sound so skeptical?"

"Why is your face turning bright red?"

It did no good for Piper to try to forget about last night's kiss—it was emblazoned on all her senses, along with today's almost kiss. She could tell herself that there had been witnesses this morning, too, that maybe Josh was keeping up the act for Daphne's sake and helping Piper make a continued point to Charlie. But deep down, she knew better. This morning hadn't been about pretense. It had been about her all but throwing herself at Josh, and his obviously recognizing the need in her eyes.

She refused to ponder what had looked like an answering need in his own. If her resolve weakened, she had a corporate no-fraternization policy and possible notches on Josh's metaphorical bedpost to help bolster it.

"Turn left up here," Daphne instructed, pointing across the street to the bridal boutique.

Today Mandy was picking up the gown she'd be wearing to her January wedding, and she'd insisted Piper drop by to see the dress while she was in town. Six years younger than Piper, Mandy had looked up to her cousin, wanted to be just like her, even saying she wanted to attend A&M university. She'd quit college midway through her degree plan, though, saying that she was spending money needlessly, since her ultimate goal was to help run the family restaurant and raise kids. Piper hadn't seen her cousin in years or met Mandy's fiancé, Donald.

Parking the car, Piper squirmed a little as she thought about the number of times she'd made excuses not to visit her family.

It wasn't that she didn't love them, she thought as she and Daphne entered the bridal boutique. She just didn't want to live the life they'd envisioned for her.

Inside, lacy reminders of that life surrounded her. Veils and cake toppers and tiny wedding favors that made her shudder deep inside. At the handful of weddings she'd attended, she always flinched when a bride promised to "love and obey."

Glancing past the racks of white and ivory accessories for the ceremony, she saw that the back of the store was stocked with silk nighties and crystal vials of perfume for the wedding night. Her breath rippled out of her in a lusty sigh. Although she couldn't quite picture herself at the front of a church pledging her life to a man, it was disturbingly easy to imagine Josh carrying her over the threshold of a honeymoon suite where they'd make love all night.

Daphne led Piper past a platform surrounded by mirrors to a row of dressing rooms. Mandy stood outside one of the small rooms with her sister, Stella, and their mother.

"Piper!" Mandy rushed forward for a hug. "I haven't seen you in ages!"

Mandy's mother stood to the side, her lips pursed. "We weren't sure you'd make it."

"I said I would."

Her aunt sniffed. "Yes, well. Come on, Mandy. Go ahead and try on your dress."

Mandy happily ducked into one of the dressing rooms, accompanied by one of the boutique's attendants.

"You know," Stella remarked to no one in particular, "I don't even know why she went through the expense of buying a dress. I have three perfectly good ones, and I told her she could take her pick."

Stella was a victim of the warped a-woman-isn't-complete-without-a-man philosophy. As a result, she'd made hasty marital decisions to avoid being alone.

Piper whispered to her sister, "Stella seeing anyone these days?"

"No. Come to think of it, she'll be 'uncoupled' at the

shower, too, so Charlie will help round things out. She didn't want to come, but as the sister of the bride..."

Piper started to say that there was no shame in being single, citing herself as an example, but then realized she couldn't. As far as her family knew, she was with Josh. Still, her feminist ideals refused to be completely contained.

"Has anyone told Stella that there's nothing wrong with not having a man in her life?"

Daphne raised an eyebrow. "Of course there's nothing wrong with not having a man in your life. But think about how happy Josh makes you. Stella just wants that happiness, too. She's lonely."

"Loneliness is no reason to get married three times."

"Well, no, but there are plenty of great reasons to get married. You guys talking about it at all yet?"

"You sound like Mom." Piper had meant it to be a joke, but there was more accusation than humor in her words. And they both heard it.

"Something you want to get off your chest?" Daphne demanded.

This was hardly the time or place, but since it had come up.... "You threw me last night with your decision to stay at home with the twins. That isn't like you."

Her sister scowled. "First of all, I haven't made a final decision yet. Second, as little as you bother to call or visit these days, you don't know what's like me. Third, you're a damn hypocrite."

"Excuse me?" Piper knew her aunt and Stella were shooting curious glances their way, but she was unable to keep her voice from rising slightly.

"You and your talk about women having more

choices. Am I only entitled to make choices if they're the ones *you'd* make?"

"Of course not!"

"Really? Because you seem awfully judgmental of anyone who—"

"Okay," a voice from the dressing room chirped at them, "this is it." The door swung open and Mandy emerged, turning to Piper. "What do you think?"

Hardly seeing the dress, Piper made an automatic "it's gorgeous" response. The truth was, she didn't know *what* to think anymore.

SANDWICHED IN A PICKUP truck between Piper's father and ex-boyfriend, Josh gritted his teeth as they made their way down what could only loosely be called a street. Mr. Jamieson, claiming there was no use having a truck if you couldn't take the roads less traveled, said the back way would get them to the other side of town faster. Not that Josh was in any hurry to join the Jamieson women at a bridal-baby shower.

At least the shower would mean his time alone with Charlie and Mr. Jamieson was almost over. They'd played a couple hands of poker—during which Josh had been more than happy to win some of the mayor's money—and Mr. Jamieson had then pulled out a family album, showing Josh childhood pictures of Piper, which Josh fully intended to tease her about later. Still, the morning had been uncomfortable. Charlie had inserted a number of observations as he glanced over Josh's shoulder at photographs.

"I remember that picture—a high school dance. In college, we used to go dancing practically every week.

Lord, that woman can move. You guys go out dancing a lot?''

Not that Charlie had paused in his Piper-and-I remembrances long enough for Josh to ever answer a supposed question about his own relationship with her. Since Piper's parents, for whatever unfathomable reason, liked Charlie, Josh had refrained from being openly hostile to the mayor while under the Jamiesons' roof. Piper's father had compensated with his own friendly acceptance, but that had only made Josh feel guilty over his lie to her family. Every time Piper's dad called him "son" in that accepting manner, Josh's deception seemed a bit less innocent.

They think I care about Piper.

He cared about her. Just not in that white-picket fence way the Jamiesons thought she deserved. What they didn't seem to realize was that Piper would go stir-crazy behind a white-picket fence. Still, if she ever did decide to let a man into her life, she deserved one who could commit to her fully.

One like Charlie?

The thought was more painful than the bone-jarring jolt of the pickup bouncing through another pothole big enough to warrant its own zip code.

It wasn't only Josh's dislike for the mayor that made him reject the idea of Piper and Charlie. Josh had never felt possessive of a woman before, but the thought of Piper with *any* man… *You never should have kissed her.* It had done nothing to sate his hunger for her.

On the contrary, the incident in her parents' kitchen had only whetted an appetite he'd fought for months to deny. The memory of Piper's kiss had kept him up all night.

A smarter man would have learned his lesson from that kiss, backed away, regrouped—the way he'd tried to last night, when he'd gone back to his own room unkissed and rock hard. But this morning, Josh had found himself once again weakening in the face of temptation, as unwise as a moth darting gleefully into a flame. He'd jumped into the fire with both feet, tormenting himself by teasing Piper. Kissing the curve of her neck? Suggesting body lotions? He'd behaved with all the self-preservation instincts of a lemming.

A year ago, his flirting with her had been a harmless habit. He reasoned that if he stopped now, she'd know something was wrong. Besides, he enjoyed bantering with her. The flush in her cheeks, the way her turquoise eyes glimmered, never knowing ahead of time whether she'd give him hell right back or get embarrassed... This morning, he would have sworn her reaction had been arousal.

Aroused? The same woman who'd called their kiss last night "no big deal"? Suddenly, a relationship that had always been clear-cut was full of mixed signals and potential land mines.

"So, son," Fred Jamieson began, startling Josh from his frustrated thoughts. "Tell me about this sideline contracting you do."

Josh expounded on his business gratefully, glad to be thinking about more wholesome activities. As he spoke, he became slowly aware of just how successful the freelancing was, generating so much extra work that it had the potential to become a second full-time job if he let it. Maybe his being so busy with work was why he hadn't dated much lately.

Yeah, you keep telling yourself that, buddy.

Oh, he dated. But at some indefinable point his dates had started ending with alarmingly G-rated exchanges. Maybe an occasional PG-13 slipped in there from time to time, but it had been too damn long since he'd had a really good R-rated evening.

Mr. Jamieson muttered something about having to attend a girls' party, then clapped Josh on the arm. "Hell of a way to spend the afternoon, isn't it? But Astrid would have my hide if I missed it. I am terrified of that woman." His tone made it clear he was nuts about her.

"I know how you feel," Josh commiserated.

Piper's father grinned. "I believe you do, son. I believe you do."

PIPER DRUMMED HER FINGERS on the armrest of her green plastic chair and glanced around the obstetrician's waiting room, which was full of women with rounded stomachs and I-could-blow-at-any-minute expressions. Most of the ladies returned her gaze with friendly smiles. The glowering woman seated next to Piper—Daphne—was the exception.

Apologizing had never been Piper's strong suit, and it was even harder to do when she still felt she had a good point. She knew Daphne had a point, too, though, and the last thing Piper had wanted was to upset her pregnant sister, putting her in a bad mood before a party in her honor.

"Daphne, I—"

"It's okay."

Piper blinked. "It is?"

"I know how much you hate saying you're sorry," Daphne said with an unexpected grin, "so I decided to spare you. Besides, it was my fault, too. Rampaging hormones and all that."

"So we're all right?"

"Yeah."

Yet despite apologies on both sides and exchanged smiles, the situation still felt strained. Unsure how to set it right, Piper was relieved when Daphne changed the subject.

"Do you mind stopping by my place for a minute when we're finished here? Blaine and I were running late this morning, and I was in a hurry to go help Mom with those cakes for the shower. I forgot Mandy's gift."

"No problem. I wanted to see the nursery, anyway."

"Great. While we're there, you can rifle through my closet and see if there's anything you want to wear."

Piper fidgeted. "What's wrong with what I've got on? The sweater's nice and the jeans are brand-new." Practically dressy for a small Texas town.

"I'm not criticizing, honest, just trying to save you from an afternoon of Mom following you around, clucking her tongue and—"

"Delivering the When Did Young Women Stop Dressing Like Women Speech."

"Exactly."

"Good point. I'll change." Wanting to seal the truce with her sister, Piper asked, "Do we have a few minutes for you to help me with my hair and makeup, too? You've always been better at that stuff than I am."

Daphne glanced at the clock over the windowed receptionist area. "As long as they get me in to see the doctor soon. The appointment itself will be over in seconds. They're just measuring me and checking the heartbeats, no sonogram today. But I have pictures...if you'd like to see them."

"Of course." She was surprised Daphne hadn't offered sooner. Just because Piper wasn't in a hurry to knit booties herself didn't mean she wasn't excited for her sister. Being an aunt might even be fun.

Daphne reached for her purse, then held out small grainy black-and-white pictures.

"This is from the very first ultrasound." Daphne's tone was thick with unshed tears that might fall at any second. "My sons. Aren't they beautiful?"

"Er, beautiful." *What am I supposed to be seeing here?* If she squinted, Piper thought she could make out a turtle.

Daphne handed her another photo. "This one they took four months later, the day they told us we were having boys."

"My God." This picture was much clearer, obviously a shot of two babies. Piper could make out profiles of tiny faces and even saw fingers on tiny hands. "Daph, I don't know what to say." Her hand went almost wistfully to her abdomen.

"I know. I'm going to be a *mom*."

"Daphne Wallace?" a nurse in a baggy uniform called out. "The doctor is ready to see you now."

Daphne struggled to pry herself out of her chair and regain her balance. Piper rose, too, following her sister and the nurse. She stood to the side while Daphne's blood pressure and weight were checked.

Piper remembered her younger sister as being so full of dreams. Daphne had talked about wanting to travel, about exotic careers. She'd wanted to be everything from a politician to an artist. Teaching was great, but now Daphne was even talking about giving that up. Was that really what she wanted?

Blaine obviously loved his wife, but Piper didn't see *him* making a lot of sacrifices. He'd inherited the family farm and gone about life as usual, while Daphne was the one bearing his children and possibly losing her career.

Piper watched as her smiling sister chatted with the nurse and described the cribs that had been selected for the twins. Daph hardly seemed filled with regret over any of her decisions. But hadn't she and Piper always said that they didn't want to end up like their mother, who had married at seventeen and never lived anywhere but Rebecca?

Mulling over the choices women in her family had made, Piper accompanied her sister into a cramped examining room where the doctor measured Daphne's ever-growing stomach. Then he pressed a white handheld device to her distended belly and a small echoing sound suddenly filled the room. *Whump whump whump whump.*

Piper turned to Daphne. "Their heartbeats?"

She nodded, eyes wide with joy.

Maternal feelings Piper hadn't known she possessed welled within her. She must have been channeling from someone else in the building. Okay, yes, there were some really great things to be said for motherhood, but there were other achievements in life, too. Like Piper's career.

Not that her job took her out on her birthday or cheered her up when her day stunk, or watched old movies with her on television. But Josh did all of that.

She'd joked before that one reason she didn't need a man in her life was because she had him.

Oh, no. What if Josh *was* the man in her life?

Ridiculous. Hormones were one thing—after this weekend, she couldn't deny Josh aroused her to a degree she'd never thought possible—but lust wasn't love. She needed to keep that in mind for her heart's sake.

8

MR. JAMIESON PARKED his truck amid the half-dozen vehicles already present outside the community hall. "Well, come on, fellas," he said in the weary voice of a soldier commanding his troops into hostile territory.

As the three men crossed the blacktop, Astrid Jamieson bustled out the main doors. "Fred, you're late!"

"Doesn't start for another twenty minutes," he contended.

"Yes," she scolded as she got closer, "but I asked you to be here forty-five minutes early to help set up, remember?"

"Would you settle for an apology and a kiss?" He scooped her into an embrace that should definitely get him out of the doghouse.

Josh and Charlie both looked away, sharing a moment of mutual discomfort and amusement.

"You guys made it." Piper's voice drifted across the parking lot.

Josh glanced up and immediately did a double take. Her radically changed appearance was like a disorienting blow to the head. She wore a blue skirt that revealed very shapely calves, and a matching sweater that made her eyes glow like the Caribbean Sea. Her hair was loose, curling against the tops of her shoulders and shining red-gold in the sun, and he'd never seen a more beautiful woman. Next to him, Charlie also gaped.

With three long strides, Josh met Piper on the sidewalk. He didn't want the mayor getting any ideas about her. Plus, Piper was *hot*—plenty of motivation for him to grab her by the waist and pull her up against him as he leaned down to kiss her.

The thoughts and feelings he'd been fighting since kissing her last night poured through him, into his actions. He traced her lips with something bordering on reverence, then delved into her mouth with emotions that were much more primal. Everything blended together in a wave of need.

After a slight gasp, Piper kissed him back, and he found the taste of her as alluring as her heady summery scent. Her tongue slid against his in an intimate caress, and desire roared through him. He pulled back slightly to suck on that lower lip he was always staring at. If they'd been alone, he would have—

Oh, hell. They weren't alone. He reluctantly broke off the kiss and looked down at the angel in his arms. She was breathing hard, her eyes unreadable. With effort, he glanced away from her flushed face and tempting lips. Everyone else had gone inside.

"Wow," Piper finally said, the single syllable more a sigh than a word.

"Yeah." NC-17 at least. And that had just been a kiss. Imagine if—no, he should *not* let himself imagine that. "You look incredible, by the way. I didn't even know you owned a skirt."

"It's Daphne's, actually." She spoke again, her voice more abrupt than dreamy. "Look, Josh, it's great of you to help me out this weekend by pretending we're a couple. Really. You don't have to kiss me like that, though. A quick peck every now and then would probably work."

Not exactly what a man liked to hear. But she was only telling him what he already knew, that they shouldn't fan the flames of the small fire that had sparked between them. He was sure now that she felt the pull of attraction, too—sure enough that he could push the issue, but why? What would happen when things didn't work out between them? And with his track record, what reason could he possibly have for believing they could work out?

He'd lost too many people. If he couldn't have Piper in his bed, he could at least keep her in his life. As long as he kept his hands to himself.

"Don't worry. I won't kiss you like that again." Yet no sooner had the words left his mouth than he found another excuse to touch her. He caught one sunset-colored curl between his fingers, and it slid over his skin like silk. "I've never seen your hair down before."

"In two years?" Her forehead puckered as she frowned. "Of course you have."

"It's always in a ponytail or braid or something."

"That can't be right. I mean, I pull it back for work and the gym, and I wear it up for dressy events, but...I never let my hair down?" She looked startled and disturbed by the discovery.

"Hey, don't get me wrong, it looks great up, too. You just took me by surprise."

"If anyone took someone by surprise here, it was you."

Surprise wasn't the only thing she'd felt, and they

both knew it. She'd been as hungry for him as he was for her, but that way lay madness.

She pivoted and began walking back toward the building, her tone as brisk and purposeful as her stride. "Everything go okay today? Dad didn't demand to know your intentions or anything, did he?"

"No. I'm sure he knows you can take care of yourself. He did ask whether we first met at the office or the apartment complex. I told him you picked me up for a one-night stand at a bar."

Her aqua eyes narrowed to dangerous slits.

"The office. I told him the office and that I love working with you. You're the most talented draftsperson I know. Besides me, of course."

A smile flirted at the corner of her mouth. "You think I'm talented?"

"You know you are." He held the door open for her. "You're the best. C, K and M is lucky to have you."

"Thanks." She sighed. "A girl likes to hear that every once in a while. This way—the room we rented is down on the left. So what did you guys do?"

"Played poker. I made thirty-six bucks. Your friend Charlie is the only politician I've ever met who can't bluff. Then your dad showed me some pictures, told me stories about you, about how a lot of your classmates went to the small college in the next county. Said that at seventeen you were ready to leave home and take on the world, that they tried to talk you into staying closer for a year or two, but you have a stubborn streak that makes mules look indecisive."

She stopped dead in her tracks, hurt in her gaze. "Are they still angry that I left?"

"I didn't get the impression that they were ever angry," he said, "just worried about you and reluctant to let go."

Did she really think her father had said anything derogatory about her? Even the mule comment had been made with paternal pride.

Piper took a deep breath. "With Mom, Dad and Daphne, I've always...I mean, the three of them... Come on, I told Mandy I'd help set up, and we're not getting anything done out here in the hall."

He followed, thinking about how ironic life could be. As he'd been shuffled from one home to the next, he'd stopped reaching out to people, stopped letting others reach him. He'd decided it would just be less painful to accept not fitting in. Was it possible that even with her close-knit family, Piper had felt like an outsider, too? Given their very different pasts, he'd never expected to have that in common with her. Didn't she know how much they cared about her?

Shaking his head, he stepped through the doorway and discovered a room decorated with balloons and crepe paper wedding bells. A garish papier-mâché stork the size of a condor hung from the ceiling, looking as though it might swoop down and attack guests.

Despite all his male instincts prompting him to flee, Josh forced his feet forward into the spacious rectangular room. At the center were several round tables. Against one wall were two tables piled with presents, and in the opposite wall was a small doorway that must lead to a private kitchen. Women of various ages entered and exited every few minutes, piling food on a large table positioned right outside the door.

Piper hurried in that direction, saying her help was needed, and left him to fend for himself. She must re-

The Harlequin Reader Service® — Here's how it works:

Accepting your 2 free books and gift places you under no obligation to buy anything. You may keep the books and gift and return the shipping statement marked "cancel." If you do not cancel, about a month later we'll send you 4 additional books and bill you just $3.57 each in the U.S., or $4.24 each in Canada, plus 25¢ shipping & handling per book and applicable taxes if any.* That's the complete price and — compared to cover prices of $4.25 each in the U.S. and $4.99 each in Canada — it's quite a bargain! You may cancel at any time, but if you choose to continue, every month we'll send you 4 more books, which you may either purchase at the discount price or return to us and cancel your subscription.

*Terms and prices subject to change without notice. Sales tax applicable in N.Y. Canadian residents will be charged applicable provincial taxes and GST.

OFFICIAL OPINION POLL

ANSWER 3 QUESTIONS AND WE'LL SEND YOU
2 FREE BOOKS AND A FREE GIFT!

0074823 ‖‖‖‖‖‖ ‖‖‖‖ ‖‖‖‖

FREE GIFT CLAIM # 3953

YOUR OPINION COUNTS!

Please check TRUE or FALSE below to express your opinion about the following statements:

Q1 Do you believe in "true love"?

"TRUE LOVE HAPPENS ONLY ONCE IN A LIFETIME."
○ TRUE
○ FALSE

Q2 Do you think marriage has any value in today's world?

"YOU CAN BE TOTALLY COMMITTED TO SOMEONE WITHOUT BEING MARRIED."
○ TRUE
○ FALSE

Q3 What kind of books do you enjoy?

"A GREAT NOVEL MUST HAVE A HAPPY ENDING."
○ TRUE
○ FALSE

YES, I have scratched the area below.

Please send me the 2 FREE BOOKS and FREE GIFT for which I qualify. I understand I am under no obligation to purchase any books, as explained on the back of this card.

DETACH AND MAIL CARD TODAY!

342 HDL DZ4A

142 HDL DZ4Q

FIRST NAME

LAST NAME

(H-T-03/04)

ADDRESS

APT.#

CITY

STATE/PROV.

ZIP/POSTAL CODE

www.eHarlequin.com

Offer limited to one per household and not valid to current Harlequin Temptation® subscribers. All orders subject to approval. Credit or Debit balances in a customer's account(s) may be offset by any other outstanding balance owed by or to the customer.

ally trust him if she didn't think he'd make a run for it as soon as her back was turned.

Blaine and a few other men sat huddled around one of the round tables, and Josh expelled a sigh of relief as he ambled in their direction. Fellow Martians on a Venusian planet. Pulling out the chair next to Blaine, he introduced himself to the others. Name tags sat in the center of the table, but none of the other guys wore a baby-bottle-shaped adhesive badge, and Josh didn't plan to be the first.

He was so relieved to be around other men that he didn't even mind too much when Charlie finished carrying a cooler for Mrs. Jamieson and joined them at the table. No guy—not even the irritating mayor—deserved to be cut adrift in this bastion of estrogen. Besides, as long as Charlie was hanging out with them, he wasn't in the kitchen, trying to corner Piper.

Blaine, who had just introduced Mandy's fiancé, asked Josh, "Have you and Piper RSVPed to the wedding yet? I was thinking that you two could stay with Daph and me instead of at a hotel. Unless you don't want twin newborns underfoot, which we would understand."

Josh gave a noncommittal smile, unbalanced by a sense of loss at never seeing these people again. Mrs. Jamieson and her great cooking, Blaine and Daphne who had warmly accepted him, Mr. Jamieson who called him "son." If his fictional relationship with Piper had actually been real, then...

He ground his teeth. Hadn't he learned long ago to stop wanting relationships? A family? Love?

If you don't want it, you can't be hurt when you don't get it. A sound outlook, but it was damn near impossible *not* to want Piper.

PIPER STOOD at the lace-covered buffet table. All the guests had arrived, and people were filling their plates with food. She breathed in the sweet, tangy smell of pineapple from the fruit salad and the zesty aroma of horseradish from the shrimp cocktail. But her stomach was still doing somersaults from that kiss in the parking lot, and she wasn't sure she could eat anything.

Darting her gaze toward a smaller table, she watched as Josh poured them both glasses of iced tea. How was it that she'd known him for so long, yet felt as though she were seeing him for the first time? She studied his profile with admiration, her knees slightly weakened by the sight of his strong jaw and teasing smile as he responded to something one of her cousins was saying. His dark hair, though not messy, was unruly above his face, as if he'd been running his hands through it. Or maybe she'd tousled it herself while they were kissing.

She shook her head, trying to forget what had happened. Yeah, right. With enough effort, she might be able to put it temporarily out of her mind, but for how long? Especially now that she knew with an unwanted certainty that their kiss last night had been anything but a fluke. She'd tried to convince herself during sleepless hours early this morning that the spontaneous combustion between them probably couldn't be duplicated a second time. But the way he'd kissed her in the parking lot had left her hot and wanting more.

Fantasies haunted her. Josh kissing her, undressing her, sharing her bed back at the hotel. It would never happen, she assured herself. But here, away from her no-men life in Houston, away from the women Josh had dated...for a second, it seemed almost possible.

Wishful thinking, prompted by hormones. She wasn't going to kid herself that a couple of steamy kisses had changed anything. Maybe if she were a different type of person, she could allow herself a weekend fling. But how could she bare herself so intimately—literally—to him, then just pretend nothing had happened when she saw him at the office on Monday? She wasn't risking their friendship, or her job, on something so brief, even if she knew the sex would be nothing short of fantastic. Somehow, though, looking around at the happy people around her—Daphne grinning at Blaine; a couple from Piper's high school class who had married after graduation but still acted like honeymooners—it was tough to remember why relationships were such bad things.

"If it isn't the Pied Piper," a voice behind her boomed. "Still short, I see."

She spun around. "Hey, Uncle Joe. Still bald, I see."

Mandy's father crushed her in a hug that must've looked to the casual observer like a mutation of the Heimlich maneuver. "I always did like you, girl. Spunky and smart. Your dad tells me you're doing pretty well for yourself up in the big city. We're all proud of you."

This was news to Piper. "I thought I was the spinster blight on the Jamieson good name?"

Before her uncle could answer, Josh reached her side, balancing a small paper plate filled with food, and two plastic cups. Piper took one of the drinks and introduced her uncle.

"Piper's mom has told us a lot about you. Pleased to meet you," Joe said, slapping Josh on the back so heartily that he lurched forward. "Let me give you two a tip—if you decide to tie the knot, *elope*. If there's one thing my daughters have taught me, it's how complicated weddings are."

Elope? Wedding? For a second, Piper's head swam. The idea of Josh settling down with *anyone* was unimaginable, much less settling down with her.

Oblivious to the mental chaos he'd caused her, her uncle glanced across the room. "If you'll excuse me, I think I'm just going to go check on your grandmother, see if she and her friend need a ride back to the nursing home when this is over."

Josh made a teasing observation about Nana's adhering to the couples theme and bringing an octogenarian suitor with her, but Piper barely heard him.

"Piper?"

She started, Josh's questioning tone interrupting the blurred, soft-focus matrimonial images that still filled her head—the traditional garter worn beneath her gown, Josh slowly rolling it down her leg, trailing his fingers against her skin.... "He was just making conversation," she said quickly.

"Hmm?"

"My uncle. The elopement advice. It was just small talk. Believe me, I didn't say anything to make my family think we were headed for the altar."

"I didn't think you did." He examined her closely. "You seem horrified by the idea. Completely appalling, huh?"

She bit her lip. If she admitted that at odd times today she'd secretly found the idea *appealing,* he'd walk straight out the door and hitchhike back to Houston.

"Yeah, well, you know. I'm not one for romance."

"Right." After a moment, he added, "We definitely see eye-to-eye there."

Once all the guests were seated and eating, Mandy and Daphne went to the front of the room with their husbands, who wore matching pained expressions. Clearly the "couples shower" concept had not been devised by men. As friends and relatives ate, Mandy unwrapped the usual bridal presents—towels and small home appliances. Then Daphne took her turn, pulling tiny baby clothes out of gift bags.

When the last package had been opened, Piper leaned closer to Josh, trying not to think about how warm and inviting his scent was as she whispered, "I don't know about you, but I'd rather not participate in the who-can-make-the-best-wedding-veil-out-of-toilet-paper games."

"That's really what women do at bridal showers?" he asked, a half smile on his face.

"In mixed company, anyway. If it were just us girls, we might still make the veils, but we'd probably also have a few drinks and encourage the bride with bawdy sex stories."

His eyes widened, but his surprised expression was almost instantly replaced with one of prurient interest. "So what's your favorite bawdy sex story?"

"Um…" Currently, the only thing that came to mind in connection with sex was the man staring back at her. "Never mind that. Let's volunteer for dish duty and escape to the kitchen while everyone else is engaged in the diapering-the-baby-doll relay or whatever."

"Sounds good to me." He stood first, pulling her chair back for her.

How many times had Josh reached past her to open her car door, or stood by as she locked her apartment? She'd noticed how tall he was on those occasions—hard not to, when he was teasing her about her own height—but this weekend she was aware of his body in a whole new way. The heat that emanated from him when he stood close, the width of his shoulders, the leisurely confidence he moved with, neither hurried nor self-conscious....

"Piper, we're kitchen-bound, right?" His tone was puzzled, and he obviously wondered why she wasn't following through on her own plan.

"R-right." They were off to wash casserole plates and punch glasses, and she wasn't going to dwell on the last time they'd done dishes together, when they'd ended up kissing. There was nothing intrinsically sexy about liquid detergent, no reason to think the incident would be repeated. Unfortunately.

Later, as she took her frustration out on a large plastic bowl coated with remnants of nacho cheese, Piper realized she needn't have worried about the sexual tension that would arise when they were alone. Josh kept himself busy loading things into the cooler at the opposite end of the kitchen or retrieving empty serving plates off the buffet table. Then Stella appeared, holding the blender Mandy had received and explaining that most of the older guests were leaving and the remaining younger ones wanted margaritas.

She mixed the first batch, delivered them and returned to make more. With her cousin's intermittent presence as unlikely chaperon, Piper managed to quit fixating on Josh long enough to finish the small pile of dishes near the sink. Finally, they were done, but Piper was in no hurry to return to the land of happy couple-dom in the other room and the uncertainty it had filled her with earlier.

Option B was to stay here with Josh. Stella had left the kitchen after making her last batch of margaritas. Piper had turned one down, figuring the drink would only jumble her thoughts further. Now, however, she was reconsidering.

Josh seemed to be enjoying his. Clearly content to be away from the shower festivities, he was leaning against the industrial-strength refrigerator behind him. Next to a very sturdy counter, she couldn't help notic-ing—one that would easily accommodate two people's weight and withstand vigorous activity.

She swallowed, wondering when she'd developed this strange countertop fetish.

Her gulp attracted his attention. He lowered the glass and met her eyes, the corner of his mouth quirked up in the sexy half grin she knew so well. "If I didn't know this weekend was a pretense, I'd never guess the look on your face was an act."

No chance in hell she was going to ask "What look?" because she knew he'd tell her. Instead, she turned the tables on him. "Just like no one would have guessed that kiss in the parking lot was an act?" She'd meant it to be a statement, not a question.

"Are you asking me if it was real?" He set his glass down and took a step closer to her. "Did you want it to be?"

Yes. No! Maybe—in a different reality. "I think we should get back out there."

"It was your idea to come in here."

"Well, yes, but not to be completely antisocial, just to escape the standard games."

"And is this another escape attempt?" He punctuated his question with an eyebrow raised in challenge.

"Escape from what, you?" She willed herself to laugh, to smile at least—anything to make light of his uncomfortably accurate insight. But she couldn't.

"Yeah, me." Stopping directly in front of her, Josh folded his arms over his chest. His stance should have relieved her, since it meant he had no immediate plans to reach for her, but she didn't feel relief. She felt like a firecracker with a fuse slowly burning down to the detonation point.

How did the man project so much untamed sensuality simply by standing there?

She forced a soft laugh. "You make it sound as if I should be scared of you." When it was really her own actions she feared. "But you're, um, perfectly harmless."

Yeah, Josh is to harmless as lion is to fluffy kitten. Any chance he hadn't noticed the quaver in her tone and the blush she could feel in her face? She braced herself for him to mention those very things, but instead he sighed.

"Well, you're right about me not harming you, anyway." His voice softened. "I would never want to do anything that could end up hurting you, Piper."

"I know you wouldn't."

Affection knotted her chest, a deep tenderness that was more disconcerting than the rampant lust. The lust she could try to attribute to months of abstinence. The wellspring of emotion wasn't as easily waved away.

He gazed at her with searing intensity, then turned to grab his margarita. "Maybe I needed the reminder myself."

As he gulped the frozen drink, Piper envied him the icy coldness and the tequila. She could use both.

Lowering the glass, he suggested, "Let's get out of here."

She followed him to safety, pondering the way he'd unexpectedly backed down. After two years of teasing her outrageously, pouncing on opportunities for innuendo, he'd let her off the hook just now. Why? Because he'd glimpsed her nervousness and was protecting her?

Or was it because their teasing had become so real that he needed to protect himself?

She had the impression that the more superficial and less genuine his relationships, the more comfortable he stayed. Instead of being relieved that they'd dodged a metaphorical bullet—or at least the mistake of getting hot and heavy among the pots and pans—she felt inexplicably sad.

Out in the main room, four couples along with Charlie and Stella remained, seated around two tables that had been pushed together. At the other end of the room, Piper's mom and aunt picked up wrapping paper and ribbon and exchanged gossip. Piper and Josh sat with the twosomes.

Daphne smiled. "Welcome back, sis. You're just in time."

"For what?"

Her sister pushed a large bag across the table to Mandy, who sat in her fiancé's lap. "We wanted to wait until it was just close friends, but we have a few presents left for Mandy and Donald. For the honeymoon," she added with a wink.

There was good-natured laughter as Donald extracted a pack of condoms with the words *Just Married* on them. Mandy retrieved the next item—a heart-shaped bottle of flavored body lotion.

"Hey!" Josh swiveled his head toward Piper. "You told me this morning we couldn't get any flavored body lotion here."

Piper felt the blood drain from her face. She imagined she was as pale as Josh had suddenly gone. Clearly, he hadn't thought before speaking. And now that all speculative gazes were locked on the two of them, he wasn't speaking at all.

Charlie reddened and said it had been nice seeing everyone, but he had to go. Stella offered to walk him out.

Daphne gave a discreet cough that no doubt covered up a laugh. "Actually, you can't buy it in Rebecca. But there's always the Web. We're not so small-town that we don't have Internet access."

"Right," Josh mumbled, his eyes fixed on the table. "Good to know."

Josh Weber, king of the suggestive insinuation, was actually *embarrassed*. Charmed by his unexpected and endearing reaction, Piper impulsively slid her hand on top of his before recalling his aversion to displays of affection. He surprised her by flipping his hand over and interlocking his fingers with hers.

Mandy once again reached into the wicked gift bag, then held up a complicated red-and-black lace contraption that perplexed Piper. How did someone who wasn't a contortionist put it on? Where did all the straps go? However one wore it, it couldn't possibly be comfortable.

But then she made the mistake of looking at Josh's face, and decided that any discomfort the garment caused would be worth it in exchange for the passion it aroused. His eyes locked with hers as he slowly traced her wrist with his thumb. He moved his fingers, sliding them up and down between hers.

Her breathing grew shallow, and she knew he could feel her pulse jumping under his thumb. He gifted her with a warm, lazy smile so intimate it made her feel as though they were the only two people in the room. When he lifted her hand and kissed it, self-preservation kicked in. She tried to pull her hand back without being too obvious.

Equally subtle and stubborn, he refused to let go.

She tugged again, and his grin widened.

"I have to go to the bathroom!" she announced loudly, yanking her hand away and springing to her feet.

Daphne stood. "I'll go with you."

Together they left the room, with Piper desperately hoping her sister wouldn't—

"So, he likes flavored body lotion?"

Oh, well. It had been an unlikely hope.

"I'm not answering that," Piper protested.

"Fine." Daphne grinned as she pushed open the door to the ladies' lounge. "I'll just have to speculate. I bet he's an incredible lover. And he's so tall, with those really big hands, that I bet—"

"Daphne!"

"Oh, come on. My hormones are in overdrive and

being this pregnant is not conducive to a love life. Let me live vicariously through you."

"To tell you the truth, Josh and I haven't...explored that area of our relationship."

"Ooh. I thought you only said you'd booked two hotel rooms to keep Dad off the warpath." She sighed deeply. "This is even better."

"Better? I thought you wanted to hear lurid descriptions of his sexual performance."

"Better for you, I mean. Don't you love this part? The long kisses that make you wonder how good his mouth will feel in other places. Staring at his hands, wondering how they'll feel against you. The anticipation that's both wonderful and maddening."

Maddening. The perfect word to describe this trip so far.

When Piper had left home on Thursday, she'd had a job she liked and a best friend who conveniently lived in her building. She hadn't been confused. No lying awake at night thinking about the way Josh kissed; no staring at sonogram pictures and trying to imagine what it would be like to have her own child growing inside her; no bridal showers where she wondered if it would really be so bad to be married.

This is why I left town in the first place, she thought as she washed her hands. *The brainwashing.*

Daphne finger-combed her dark hair and studied her reflection in the mirror, then applied a coat of lipstick. "What are you guys doing tonight? A few of us are going to that bar outside town. I may not be as light on my feet as I once was, but I can at least sit out on the deck and enjoy the music. A band from Austin's playing."

Piper hadn't thought that far ahead, but it was a sure bet she didn't want to hang out at the hotel with Josh in the adjoining room. "A night out sounds good to me if it's okay with Josh. I don't see why he'd turn down cold beer and a few hours dancing when he was willing to attend the shower."

"He was a good sport this afternoon," Daphne said approvingly. "Blaine grumbled about having to be here, and half the gifts were for us! The way Josh looks at you, he'd follow you to the end of the world."

Piper lowered her eyes, not meeting her sister's gaze in the mirror. She hated deceiving Daphne.

Oblivious to Piper's guilt, Daphne continued, "I know you said the two of you haven't discussed marriage or anything, but I doubt it will be very long before—"

"We aren't even dating," Piper confessed, desperate to shut Daphne up before her sister asked to be maid-of-honor at a nonexistent wedding. "Josh isn't my boyfriend."

Her sister turned, leaning against the marbled vanity. "That's ridiculous."

"I told Mom I had a date just to get her off my back, and she assumed I was seeing someone. So Josh, who is a good friend but *nothing more*, agreed to come with me this weekend and be that 'someone'."

"You're kidding."

"I'm really not."

"You lied to me?" Daphne's eyes clouded with hurt. "I know Mom can get carried away and drive you nuts, but we used to be really close. Why didn't you just tell me the truth?"

"I'm sorry."

Her sister sighed. "It's okay. It might've started as a fib, but from what I've seen between you this weekend, I guess you're a couple now. Ironic, huh?"

"No." Her family gave new definition to the word *stubborn*. "Hear what I'm telling you, Daph. We're *not* a couple, so there's not any irony." *And Dad says I'm mulish?*

"This is your sister you're talking to. I see how you look at him."

Not this again—Josh had been remarking on the same thing in the kitchen. "All right, you caught me. He's easy on the eyes. Can't a girl do some harmless ogling?"

Daphne stared at her, a faintly pitying you-really-don't-know-do-you expression settling over her features. Then she laughed. "Not that part, the other kind of looking. Piper, you're in love."

9

HOURS LATER, Piper still couldn't get the ridiculous claim out of her head. Darn Daphne's overactive imagination. *You're in love.*

"I am not," she assured her reflection.

The woman staring back from the hotel room mirror didn't look convinced.

Forget about that and just finish getting ready. Easier said than done. Everyone had been too full from the food at the shower to handle a sit-down dinner, so she and Josh had had more than enough time to return to the hotel and get ready to go out tonight. At least, it would have been enough for a woman who hadn't applied, washed off and reapplied her makeup, not to mention changed clothes a ridiculous number of times.

She could blame Daphne for that, too. When they'd stopped at Daph's place earlier, her sister had given her several like-new outfits. Piper had laughingly argued that Daphne would probably fit into these again someday, even if it didn't seem like it now, but her sister had said the clothes would be out of style by then and besides, this gave her an excuse for future shopping. Now, Piper had entirely too many wardrobe choices.

Recalling Josh's blatant admiration this afternoon, she had first toyed with the idea of wearing a skirt tonight. Then annoyance had seeped through her system like a noxious liquid. That kind of change, though admittedly small, had been how things started to go wrong with Charlie. And at least he'd been willing to spend his life with her. She rarely knew ahead of time if Josh would be spending his lunch hour with her.

Discarding the skirt, she'd tried to split the difference by putting on comfortably worn jeans but wearing sexy makeup and her hair loose. Then she'd realized that was stupid. Even though the covered patio-style bar would be nice and cool tonight, dancing would warm her up considerably and possibly have her makeup smudged and her hair limp. Besides, did she really think it was a good idea to do anything that could be construed as sexy? No.

What a sorry state she was in—she didn't want to attract Josh, but apparently wanted to look noticeably great around him, all the same. Weird twisted female logic.

Not as twisted as the idea that you might be in love with him.

Well, she wasn't, she told herself as she yanked her hair up into a bouncy ponytail. Luckily, the cheerful, curly end result didn't reflect the mood she'd been in while styling. She limited her makeup to some color around her eyes and shiny gloss that promised "kissable lips." Just a figure of speech, written by some schmo in a marketing department somewhere. It had nothing to do with the course of her evening. For clothes, she went back to the crisp black jeans she'd started with this morning, accompanied by a snazzy little red sweater with cap sleeves and a scooped neckline that had more of a dip than her usual tops. She had the benefit of feeling sexy, but could still tell herself she hadn't gone to any extra trouble. The sweater was simply a smart choice for not getting overheated in the crowded bar.

Just as she was telling herself she'd finally achieved the right look—casual hotness—a knock sounded at the door, the safe one that led to the hallway.

"Be there in a sec." She crossed the room and opened the door.

Josh was a study in contrasting denim. His long-sleeved shirt looked soft to the touch and was much lighter than the dark blue jeans cut from a heavier material. A look well-suited to the bar they were headed for, but did he have to wear a button-down shirt? All she could think about was the night before, watching him unbutton those last few buttons and wishing she'd been the one to do it for him.

"Hey." His smile and tone were the same ultracasual he'd adopted on the drive to the hotel. "Ready to go?"

After they'd left the shower, conversation between them had been constant and trivial—a lot of talk with absolutely nothing said. But they'd avoided enigmatic silences, difficult topics and flirting of any kind. He was standing by his earlier retreat in the community center kitchen. A wise course of action.

And she was a fan of wisdom, Piper reminded herself as she followed him down the hotel staircase, observing that men like Josh were the reason jeans had been invented. She was wise enough to know that she wasn't in love, anyway. What had happened this weekend was an anomaly, easily explained. She and Josh had been spending too much time together lately. He was a sexy man, and her repressed hormones were rebelling. Seeing him here, at her home, around her family, lent an intimacy to their relationship that hadn't been there at ball games or the local pizza joint. All of that was circumstantial; it wasn't love. Except...

She bit her lip as he unlocked the car doors. Hadn't she been the one to think that he should find a nice girl, that he had more to offer than a few nights of fun? Yet the thought of him settling on one woman made her skin crawl. Josh and Gina were two of her very favorite people, but earlier this week, the idea of the two of them together had hurt.

You're just afraid of being displaced if he ever found a lasting relationship.

Maybe that really was what bothered her, she told herself moments later, as they drove down the dark rural stretch of highway. She *was* jealous, but not in a sexual or romantic sense, simply a possessive he's-my-best-friend-and-I-don't-want-to-lose-him way. Funny, but she didn't think she and Charlie had ever had that.

There'd been the thrill of falling in love and the thrill of her first sexual exploration, but there'd never been deep friendship. In retrospect, the best part of their physical relationship, for her anyway, had been the sense of discovery, the short-lived novelty of feeling that she was somehow more fully a woman. Sex had been okay, but she hadn't experienced a burning desire for her fiancé. Not like the desire she'd been feeling for Josh the last few days.

She might try to tell herself Josh was just a friend, but she'd never wanted anyone the way she wanted him.

Gina's words from earlier in the week taunted her. Her friend seemed to think Josh just hadn't found the right woman. Was that true? And if so, did Piper want to be that woman?

Glad for the nighttime that hid her pensive expression, she said, "While we're alone, I just wanted to say thank you again for coming with me this weekend. I hope it's no trouble."

"Nope. And you're welcome." The glowing dashboard panel illuminated his quick smile, his teeth flashing white.

"I can't believe you were even free...what with working your sideline projects. And all your dating."

He didn't say anything, and Piper experienced a moment of self-loathing. What was she doing here? Shamelessly fishing?

She knew there had been dozens of women in his life; she just didn't know what part they'd played. Had he slept with all of them, or did some of his dates end platonically? Hard to believe, when the man oozed the promise of sexual fulfillment. Had he loved any of the women he'd known? Had he ever been hurt by a woman?

The truth was, all Piper had were unsubstantiated guesses based on his teasing remarks and the roster of female Houstonites who accosted him while he was out in public. But the fact that she saw Josh almost every single day, considered him her best friend and didn't know much beyond Michelle had a cat and Nancy wanted to see him again reminded Piper of how private he was.

Suddenly, she needed more information. "I was just wondering...you *do* date an awful lot."

"That isn't a question."

He didn't sound angry, so she pushed bravely—or stupidly—forward. "Well, you do, don't you?"

Another grin flashed, this one quicker than the last before it dissolved into the darkness. "I figure I have to date enough for the both of us in order to maintain cosmic balance."

Classic Josh Weber answer—entertaining and evasive. This was what he did, kept people at bay without their even realizing it, smiling and cracking jokes the entire time.

Piper didn't want to be kept at bay anymore. She wanted to know what the risks were, wanted to see his life with open eyes so that she could determine if there was room in it for another person. And so she could force herself to accept the situation once and for all if there wasn't.

"I know you're going to say this is none of my business, but I...I care about you, as your friend. If you want to be left alone, why do you date all the time? And if you do want to be with someone, then..."

"Then what?" he countered, his tone a defensive challenge.

"You're going to have to change."

He swiveled his head to look at her, and she couldn't see the anger in his expression so much as feel it. "Funny. Most women like me the way I am, Piper."

Ain't that the truth. "I'm surprised you can conclude how they feel about you, given your tendency not to stick around."

"Where do you get off implying that I can't be there for someone? I'm here now, aren't I? And I believe I've commented before on the irony of you giving me dating advice. At least *I'm* not hiding in my work."

Ouch. Of all the people in her life, she'd thought Josh had some idea of how important her job was to her. "I'm not hiding! If anything, you're the one who's hiding—in plain sight, as the saying goes. You give the illusion of going from one relationship to the next, but you don't let people get close to you, so you're actually more alone than I am."

Josh couldn't help flinching, but he doubted she'd noticed. She seemed to be on quite the roll. He didn't know what the hell had brought this on, but whether she'd meant to hit such a raw nerve or not, he wanted her to stop. Immediately.

"Are you finished, or are you auditioning for your own talk show? 'Do as I Say, Not as I Do' with our host, Dr. Piper."

"That's not fair."

"Neither is ambushing someone you call a friend. What do you know about being alone, Piper?"

She had friends in Houston who met every need, from workout buddy to this lunatic weekend of fooling her family. And then there was her family itself. Sure, her relatives could be overbearing at times, but they adored her. They all seemed so happy that she'd finally come home that he half expected a parade in her honor. The first person Josh had ever truly considered spending his life with, Dana, was now a bittersweet memory; the first person Piper had ever considered spending her life with was still hanging around hoping she'd change her mind.

"I—"

He couldn't take any more of this. "It was a rhetorical question." To make sure he got his point across, he flipped on the car stereo, letting the angry cadence of a hard rock song stoke his indignation.

This was what he got for kissing her—being talked to death. Didn't they have a good time as friends? Didn't she enjoy his company and know she could count on him? Why wasn't that enough? Women. What was with the quest for details, the need to have a man spill his emotions? Thank God he hadn't slept with her.

Yet even as he had the thought, he was forcibly reminded of the arousal he'd been fighting. As ticked off as he was at the moment, the unique scent of her teased him—as did the thought that sex after an argument could be the best sex of all. Sure, making love to Piper would be a huge mistake, one he'd managed to so far avoid, but if the opportunity really presented itself, he didn't think he could pass it up. Mistake or not.

True to form, Piper ignored his attempted retreat. She reached out and switched off the radio. When he glared in her direction, he saw the stubborn set of her jaw and the way her arms were crossed over her chest. It was a crime to flatten breasts like hers.

Despite himself, he almost smiled at her feisty demeanor. At the moment she was being a real pain in the ass, but the way Piper refused to back down was something he lov— He admired that in her. "You had something you wanted to add, no doubt?"

"Yeah. An apology. I keep telling my mom to butt out of my love life—"

"You don't have a love life." He hadn't yet forgiven her enough to pass up the small jab.

"Anyway, if I'm happy single, why shouldn't you be? What a hypocrite I turned out to be."

Josh wondered if she even knew how wistful her expression had grown at the bridal shower earlier. For just a minute, she'd seemed enchanted by the idea of her own wedding. Or maybe she'd just been enchanted by the idea of a well-deserved vacation on the beaches of sunny Cancun, the bride and groom's honeymoon destination. Hard to believe Piper might really want to get married, but until a few days ago, Josh wouldn't have believed she'd relentlessly pry into his private life, either.

"Are you happy?" he asked. "Being single, I mean?"

She studied his face in the darkness. "Aren't you?"

"Absolutely."

"Yeah. Me, too."

THERE WAS QUITE A CROWD gathered at the bar. People were in the mood to appreciate the live music and semi-outdoor venue now that the sweltering Texas summer had finally ended. Also, Piper supposed that, for anyone who had already seen both movies showing at the cinema and didn't feel up to some Friday-night cow-tipping, there weren't a whole lot of social alternatives. The bass from the band shook the ground beneath her feet as she followed Josh across the small, overflowing parking lot. Trucks with four-wheel drive and tires equipped for "mudding" had made their own parking in the field next to the building. Patrons waiting in line outside chatted and laughed, some tapped their feet to the boisterous George Strait classic being played. In contrast, Josh's perfunctory smile was subdued.

She'd hurt him. For just a second, even in the darkness of the car, she'd glimpsed actual pain in Josh's eyes. She never should have said that to him about being alone. He wasn't someone who held a grudge, but things hadn't been the same between them since their earlier conversation. Whatever she'd been trying to accomplish—and she was fuzzy on that in hindsight—she'd failed.

When it was their turn in line to pay the cover charge, she pushed a ten across to the cashier, waving away Josh's five. "It's the least I can do." She wasn't sure whether she meant she owed him for this weekend or for her earlier outburst.

They walked inside, through the smaller interior of the club, where the rectangular bar took up the center of the room and customers shot pool or played darts. Beyond that was a door leading out to the oversize deck area and covered dance floor. A band played on a dais, and tables were scattered off to the sides along gazebo-like trellises. Piper opened the door, scanned the crowd and finally spotted Mandy, once again perched in her fiancé's lap.

"This way," Piper told Josh, taking a shortcut across the edge of the oval dance floor underneath the strings of multicolored lights.

The twang of the guitars in the band and the mingled scents of cologne and beer filled her with nostalgia. She'd left Rebecca too young to get into any of the area bars, but no self-respecting Aggie graduated from A&M without going to a few beer joints and dance halls.

Mandy beamed in greeting. "I'm really glad you're here this weekend, Piper. The rest of my family's been driving me nuts."

"I know the feeling," Piper said.

"Stella's after me to ask this man we barely know to be a groomsman just so she has an excuse to get close to him, and my mother is speculating about everything that could go wrong with the wedding. I swear we should elope."

Donald patted his fiancée's hand. "It'll be all right, dumplin'. In a few months, the wedding will be behind us, and we'll be in Cancun."

Piper nodded. "Wise man." Even if he did call his bride-to-be 'dumplin'."

"Piper!" Daphne was winding her way through the crowd at a rapid clip, her grimly determined expression incongruous with the lively atmosphere. As Blaine caught up with her, Daphne explained breathlessly, "I was trying to hurry. I wanted to warn you that—"

"Hi there." Charlie Conway's voice, melodious enough for public speaking, was beginning to sound to Piper like fingernails on a chalkboard.

"Too late," Daphne muttered.

Piper sighed. "Hello, Charlie."

He pushed past Daphne and Blaine, sparing Josh a civil nod before extending an upturned palm in Piper's direction. "I was hoping for a dance."

Why couldn't he accept that there would never be anything between them again? Was it simply because Rebecca's golden boy wasn't used to taking no for an answer? "You know I'm here with Josh."

Charlie managed to look wounded. "And he won't let you share one dance for old time's sake?"

Let? She had to give Charlie credit—he knew which buttons to push. Then again, why wouldn't he? Toward the end of their ill-fated relationship, he'd pushed all the wrong ones.

But in their years together, they had shared some good times. Given the high points of their past and the nostalgia she'd been feeling, it seemed churlish to refuse one simple dance. She glanced toward Josh, who didn't meet her gaze. If he was still angry about her earlier comments in line, maybe some distance would do them both good. She owed him some space.

"*One* dance," she finally agreed.

Flashing a dimpled smile that made him look nineteen for a second, Charlie took her hand to lead her onto the floor. Strange that there had once been a time when he...what—made her heart race? Piper wondered. Try though she might, she couldn't recall ever feeling the exhilaration, frustration and sheer desire a single glance from Josh could incite. Had she ever truly loved the man she'd once planned to marry?

She absently matched his movements, not needing to concentrate to do so. The two of them had shared so many dances that she knew instinctively when he would turn and what steps he would take.

"We still move together as if we were one person," Charlie murmured in what was probably supposed to be a seductive, husky whisper. But he was trying too hard. Real seduction was inexorable, deriving its very power from a sense of inevitability, not effort.

She moved back, putting distance between them. "It's not very hard to predict what you're going to do, Charlie. You haven't updated your moves since you were a teenager."

"Don't be so sure." The way his thigh brushed hers

as they turned was probably not an accident. "I've got some more adult ones now."

Piper almost laughed. His forced attempts at flirtation bordered on the comical when contrasted to her time with Josh.

Speaking of Josh...she shot pleading glances over Charlie's shoulder. She'd thought that a quick dance and a stroll down memory lane would be bearable, but now she wanted to flee. Josh had always been fairly well attuned to what she was thinking—maybe he'd help her out.

Or not.

Blond and beautiful Rosalyn Granger, a woman who'd been in the same grade as Piper, stood by Mandy's table, introducing herself to Josh. Piper could see the interest in the woman's eyes even from this distance. Josh smiled, said something that was no doubt charming, and Rosalyn laughed. Then she touched his arm—the universal sign of a woman flirting.

Piper wondered if the two of them would go dance together. *I'll bet Roz won't start telling him how to live his life, and tick him off.* Even though Josh hadn't made a move in Rosalyn's direction, the image of him taking her into his arms on the dance floor was imprinted so hard on Piper's brain her head hurt from it.

Rosalyn finished whatever she was saying, then touched his arm again. Really, had the woman no shame?

"Could you excuse me, Charlie?" In a complete breach of etiquette, Piper abandoned her partner in the middle of a song. She hurriedly crossed the room, skidding to a stop between Josh and Rosalyn.

Pasting the biggest possible grin on her face, Piper

exclaimed, "Roz! What a nice surprise to see you here! You look great." Dammit.

Rosalyn's answering smile lacked enthusiasm. "I saw you out on the floor with Charlie. You two still make the cutest couple. We've all been wondering when you'll get back together."

When hell freezes. "Charlie and I are just old friends. My heart belongs to Josh here." She squeezed his hand for emphasis.

"Hey, Roz, is that you?" A guy just walking through the doorway called out a greeting, and with one last sultry smile for Josh, Rosalyn ambled away.

"Piper, about my hand," Josh said. "You're cutting off the circulation."

Disgusted with herself, she promptly let go. He wasn't really her boyfriend; no reason to act like a possessive lover.

"Sorry," she muttered. Her gaze collided with Daphne's, who watched from her seat at the table.

Her sister glanced from Josh to Piper, then smirked.

I am not in love with him, Piper broadcasted the message with sibling telepathy and a strong glare. *We are just friends.*

Sure you are. Daphne's sarcastic thoughts were as easy to read as the neon blue beer sign blinking on the latticed wall behind her.

Glancing away from her sister, Piper looked up at Josh and wondered at the source of his fierce scowl. Was he angry that she'd run off Rosalyn? Or still annoyed about their earlier conversation?

"What's wrong?" she asked him.

"You tell me." He crossed his arms. "I'm not the one

who barreled over here to snap at an old school buddy. Looked to me like you were jealous.''

"Jealous? Ha! You're clearly not getting enough oxygen to your brain." She tilted her head back. "The air you're breathing way up there must be too thin. If I seem annoyed, it's just because we had a deal." Lowering her voice, she added, "Our relationship might not be real, but I'd appreciate you not picking up other women in front of my family."

"Rosalyn was just keeping me company while *you* were out there in the arms of your ex-fiancé."

His tone was so biting, so un-Joshlike, that she blinked. Despite the accusation he'd tossed at her, was it possible *he* was jealous? And if he were, what did that mean?

Not this again. Honest to heaven, she wasn't one of those women who stood around analyzing men and feelings and relationships. At least, she never had been before. Grinding her teeth, she recalled times she'd congratulated herself on not obsessing about a guy the way some women did. How the mighty had fallen.

She needed a distraction. "Let's dance."

"Fine." His hand around hers was gentle enough, but his posture suggested they were about to enter into hand-to-hand combat instead of the Texas version of the waltz.

10

DESPITE JOSH'S CUSTOMARY grace and her vast experience dancing, they trampled each other's toes and risked banging into each other whenever they turned corners.

"I thought you knew how to dance," she grumbled.

"I do." He shot her such a pointed look that she bristled.

"Are you saying I don't? If you'd been watching when Charlie and I were dancing, you'd know that—"

"Charlie let you lead. Say what you want about me and my need for control, Piper, but I'm not the only one."

"I..." Dammit, he was right.

Not just about the dancing, either. She liked being in charge of her life, dreaded the thought of a man trying to muscle in. She guarded her autonomy by keeping men at arm's length.

But this was just a dance floor, for heaven's sake. Surely she wasn't such a control freak that she couldn't let Josh lead? Inhaling deeply, she forced herself to relax and follow him. As it grew easier to move her body in rhythm with his, she began to enjoy the physical give and take, the way their movements brought them closer together and then apart just long enough to make her yearn to be against him again.

Gradually unwinding, Piper smiled up at him and

even hummed along with the band. Josh grinned back, obviously taking her sacrificed lead as the apology it was. When the song ended, Josh's fingers, interlocked with hers, loosened their grip slightly, and he hesitated.

Piper tilted her head back. "I'm game to stay out here a while longer if you are. I love to dance." Which was true, but more than that, she needed the physical outlet for the emotional frustration she'd been feeling.

The dancing couldn't help alleviate the sexual frustration, though. That only grew worse as Josh pressed his other hand against her hip to guide her in a turn. They did several tight spins together, his long legs grazing hers, the denim he wore making a raspy whisper. When the music shifted to a ballad, Piper's heart fluttered. Slow dancing with Josh seemed a dangerous idea, but she'd just finished saying she didn't want to quit anytime soon.

They both stilled for a second, and Piper stared at his shirt, not wanting to meet his gaze. Then he pulled her closer to him, so that she could have rested her cheek against his chest. Josh lifted her hand, moving it so that it cupped his neck, and dropped his own hand to join the other at her waist. Plenty of couples around them had adopted this exact stance, but that didn't keep the situation from feeling blatantly intimate. Arms around him, she scooted closer, moving her feet absently, mostly just swaying now. With every brush of their bodies, Piper's blood heated. Her breasts pressed lightly against him, just enough to tease her senses, and lower, between her thighs, the part of her that so desperately wanted to be pressed against him, ached with damp need. It occurred to Piper that with her fingers laced behind the nape of his neck and his hands at her hips, resting at the sensitive space just atop the curve of her bottom, she and Josh were nearly in the same position they'd been in when they'd kissed earlier.

All she had to do was look up.

Josh swallowed. "I know you wanted to dance, but...it's gotten kind of crowded out here."

She clung to the excuse to escape. "Yeah, everyone comes out for the slow stuff."

"How about we take a break? I could grab us a couple of cold beers."

She nodded in prompt agreement. Then, eager to sit for a while, she rejoined Daphne at the table.

"Hey," her sister said. "We were just debating how much longer to stay. I tire out pretty easily these days, and I want to conserve energy for all that shopping tomorrow."

Piper grinned. Tomorrow afternoon was the reunion picnic, and most of her relatives would be at the Rebecca Fall Festival in the morning. But Blaine, Piper and Daphne had attended dozens of past festivals, and Piper had suggested the four of them visit an outlet mall a couple of counties over instead. Daphne had been thrilled by the suggestion of one last pre-baby shopping spree; Blaine, while not as thrilled, had the good sense to humor his heavily pregnant wife.

They'd be back in time for the reunion, and this way Piper wouldn't spend the day on old-fashioned carnival rides with Josh. If she couldn't even wash dishes with the man without wanting to peel his clothes off, then she had no business going through the dimly lit Tunnel of Love with him, or being seat-belted into the cozy seat that would take them to the top of the Ferris wheel.

As though Daphne knew exactly who Piper was thinking about, she asked, "Where's Josh?"

"Grabbing us a couple of beers." She glanced around to make sure he was still out of earshot. "I don't know what to do about him, Daph."

"Jump him." her sister offered helpfully. "I did mention my hormones are in overdrive lately, right?"

Earlier that day, Piper would have protested that the idea was crazy. She and Josh were friends. He left a wake of broken hearts as wide as the Rio Grande. And the last thing she needed was a man complicating her life. So why wasn't she scoffing at Daphne's suggestion?

Instead, the suggestion took on a life of its own in Piper's imagination. Josh kissed with a slow, sure thoroughness that suggested he knew how to show a woman a good time. An unselfish, unhurried, uninhibited *very* good time.

He arrived at the table just in time to catch what Piper was sure was a fire-engine-red blush, but he didn't say anything as he handed her a frosty brown glass bottle. His fingers brushed hers, and heat swelled in her body, making her feel tight and full in places she'd almost forgotten about until this weekend.

She quickly gulped her beer, but it didn't help. She guzzled a bit more than she intended, and choked.

Josh handed her a napkin. "Are you all right? You're..."

Acting like a lunatic, she silently finished for him. Prying into stuff they never discussed, swooping down on Rosalyn like something out of *Fatal Attraction*, insisting he dance with her, then fighting with him over who got to lead.

To say nothing of the way she kept undressing him with her eyes.

"I'm fine." Piper sipped her beer. Slowly.

Fine? She was tense around the one person with whom she'd always been able to relax. This was Josh, the guy who let her vent about work and constantly borrowed her fabric softener because he liked the brand, but didn't want to be seen buying a bottle with a teddy bear on the label. Couldn't they go back to that—to the easy camaraderie they'd shared? She so desperately wanted to say the right thing, to restore the normalcy of their comfortable relationship.

Preparing for the casual one-liner or friendly observation that would point them in the right direction, she cleared her throat, opened her mouth to speak. But nothing came out. She was at a loss.

Seeking inspiration, she turned to face him. Her gaze locked with his, and his green-gold eyes sent shivers up her spine. The only things she was inspired to do had nothing to do with conversation. Openmouthed with nothing to say, she nervously cleared her throat again and gave a little cough.

"You sound like you're coming down with a sore throat," Josh commented solicitously. He looked almost hopeful, as though illness and a possible fever would explain the way she'd been acting.

Talk about a blow to her pride. Only moments ago she'd been thinking about this man in strictly sexual terms, while he looked ready to run right out and buy her a box of tissues and a bottle of vitamin C.

"N-no, I'm healthy as a horse." Now she was comparing herself to livestock? Good thing she'd made a conscious choice to be celibate, because she clearly lacked feminine wiles.

"Piper?" Charlie Conway approached the table. Nuisance though he was, his presence at least put an end to her making a fool of herself. For now. "You walked off, so we never really had our dance. I thought maybe now—"

"Sure." Anything to get away from the sexy man sitting next to her, confusing her so much that white-jacketed men with butterfly nets couldn't be too far off in her future. But this time, she was going to use the opportunity to set Charlie straight.

Thankfully, the band was playing a fast song, which allowed her to move constantly and not get too close to him.

He licked his lips nervously. "Piper, I've realized nothing I say is going to convince you that we belong together. So I'm not going to try to convince you with words." He stopped suddenly, leaning in.

She realized with a sort of detached horror that he was lowering his head to kiss her. *The only man I want kissing me is Josh Weber.* Even though Daphne had tried to warn her, the truth was so forceful that for a moment Piper couldn't move. *I love him. I'm in love with Josh.*

"Stop!" Belatedly mobilizing herself, she shoved Charlie away. "Enough is enough. I didn't want to have to be rude about this because we're old friends, but I don't want you. You don't want me, either. You want the perfect Rebecca housewife next to you during your mayoral campaigns."

"That's not true," he protested. He rocked back on his heels, running a hand through his blond hair. "I'll admit, maybe it was at one time. I did try to change you, but I'm older now, Piper. Smarter. I know what I lost. I've had plenty of time to find 'the perfect Rebecca housewife,' but that's not what I want."

Unfortunately, we don't always get what we want. "I'm with Josh now." She'd repeated that sentence, or variations thereof, so many times this weekend. Only this time did the irony bite her on the ass. She *wasn't* with Josh, but she wanted to be.

Charlie regarded her for a long moment. "You care that much about him?"

Lord help her, she did. She'd always imagined that love made a woman less, somehow, but thinking about all the times she'd spent with Josh, she realized he made her feel more. More confident when they discussed work, more attractive when he flirted with her, more powerful when she felt him respond to her kiss. Happier, sexier, even angrier. But never diminished in any way.

"Never mind," Charlie said. "I can see the answer in your expression. But are you sure he's the type who will stick around? I got the impression... Can he give you what you want, Piper?"

She decided to treat the question as rhetorical, since she was certain the answer was no. "Charlie, I'm sorry."

He didn't say anything when she turned and made her way back to Daphne. Josh was talking to Blaine and Donald about baseball, and Piper scooched onto the bench seat with her sister, her voice a dazed whisper.

"Daph? You were right. I am in love with him."

Daphne fluffed her dark hair. "I always was the

smart one. Piper, every time you call me, we end up talking about Josh. And with the way you smile at him, it's so obvious."

"How obvious?" Her heart pounded against her chest. "Do you think he knows?" Even Charlie had said her emotions were evident in her expression.

"No, men are clueless," Daphne assured her. "When it pertains to them, they're always the last to know. But you should tell him."

Piper sneaked a glance in his direction. The sight of him made her heart flip-flop, and she wondered if it would ever be possible to get tired of looking at him. "Tell Josh? Are you kidding? The only person in the Lone Star State more antirelationship than me?"

"I don't think of you as antirelationship, Piper. You just hadn't found the right guy to have a relationship with yet."

Piper had to admit that her views about couples and love had certainly been changing over the last few days. Still, she wasn't entirely at peace with the idea of a man taking a major role in her life again, not yet. "Daphne, if I tell you something, promise not to get mad at me?" The last thing Piper wanted was a hostile exchange like the one they'd had at the bridal shop.

Daphne waited, having had too many years' experiences as a sister to agree to a blanket promise.

Piper sighed, grateful for the thumping music of the live band that helped keep their conversation private. "You've said before that I don't want to turn out like Mom, and you're right. I respect her, and I'll admit she seems happy, but I couldn't be happy with her life."

"So who asked you to be? Falling in love doesn't need to change you into Mom or anyone els—"

"I thought it changed *you*."

"What?"

"Well, when we were growing up, you didn't sound as though you wanted to be a Rebecca housewife, either. You talked about being an artist or a politician or traveling. Then you gave it all up because of Blaine."

Instead of sounding offended, Daphne surprised her by laughing. "Piper, you took off to college when you were seventeen, and I'm almost four years younger than you. Sure, I wanted to be an artist at one time. If you'll recall, I also once wanted to be an astronaut. And I think you missed the year I wanted to start my own all-girl band. Blaine didn't change me, I just grew up, figured out what I wanted."

Piper blinked, thinking of all the times their father had expressed an opinion to which their mother had immediately agreed. Piper had imagined that Blaine and Daphne's relationship was similar. "You're not unhappy?"

"Do I *look* unhappy, you twit?" Daphne chuckled again. "Once I took some college courses, I realized teaching is my calling. I love making a difference to these kids. Plus I get summers off," she added with a teasing grin.

Piper felt confused all over again. "Then why are you talking about quitting teaching?"

"I don't plan to stop forever, just maybe take some time off while the babies are young. But even if I do turn over my classroom for a year or two, I'll still work occasionally as a sub and stay in touch that way."

"So Blaine isn't trying to turn you into Donna Reed." Piper felt about six types of stupid. She'd jumped to conclusions about her brother-in-law just because of the way Charlie had once tried to change her.

"Are you serious? Blaine likes our being a dual-income family, trust me. Piper, I don't know how you see my marriage, but if I still wanted to get into politics, my husband would personally organize my campaign against Charlie. And as for wanting to travel, we plan to, once the kids are a little older. He's not holding me back."

Piper bit her lip, afraid to open her mouth again and stick her foot any farther down her throat. Leather sandals might be great for showing off the toenails she'd painted earlier, but they made lousy snack food.

Daphne shook her head. "Mom does a lot for Dad, and you've always thought that made him some kind of chauvinist. I'm the first to admit that some of the people in this town are a little old-fashioned, but I think your view of our parents is skewed. Mom loves to cook and do things around the house. It's her domain, and she insists on controlling it. She's like you—she likes to do things her way."

Piper and her mother were alike?

"She's pushy and stubborn, but Dad's crazy about her. Half the time when she goes along with him, it's because 'his' idea was hers in the first place. You think it was Dad's choice to spend yesterday at a bridal-and-baby shower?" Daphne smiled. "Or Blaine's idea to spend tomorrow shopping? You had a bad experience with Charlie, but that's not Dad's or Blaine's fault. Or Josh's. Tell him how you feel."

Fear crowded Piper's chest, tightening her lungs. "I get that you're trying to help, but trust me, keeping this to myself is for the best. I know Josh. I understand him." And she understood he was unwilling to form any deep emotional attachments that might make him vulnerable.

Daphne arched an eyebrow. "Well, let's just hope you understand *him* better than you 'understood' my marriage."

JOSH LAY ON HIS SIDE, staring at the avocado-and-gold-paisley wallpaper illuminated by the streetlight spilling through his window. He could always pull the curtains shut, but the light outside wasn't what kept him awake. Thoughts of Piper were torturing him.

Probably just the proximity of her being curled up in bed on the other side of this wall.

Ha! She could move to Canada and he'd still be aware of her. And to be honest, it wasn't the hotel wall that separated them.

What was happening? First they'd snapped at each other earlier this evening, then she'd been so quiet on the ride back to the hotel. She'd been strangely contemplative ever since her second dance with Charlie Conway, and it made Josh uneasy. Was that why he hadn't asked what was on her mind on the return drive—fear that she was thinking about Charlie? He'd seen changes in her this weekend, despite her comments about staying single. She wouldn't reconsider Charlie's offer, would she? The mayor was downright irritating…but also apparently loyal, a more than capable provider, perhaps appealing to women and with family roots that went deep into the town's history.

She'd be miserable here. Wouldn't she? He felt as if he couldn't predict Piper as easily as he once had. Not that she'd ever been completely predictable. Banishing all nightmare-inducing thoughts of her back with Charlie, Josh stared harder at the wallpaper. Still 118 ugly swirling paisleys, same as the last four times he'd counted.

When that blonde in the bar—Rose? Robin?—had flirted with him, he'd smiled the way he normally would when an attractive woman was showing interest in him. But he'd been on autopilot, not really seeing her, attuned instead to Piper in her ex-boyfriend's arms. Charlie wasn't right for her.

But Josh wasn't right for her, either. From his business practices to his dating life, he'd remained more or less a loner, keeping his contact with others casual and as enjoyable as possible for the limited time it existed. It wasn't a bad life, so why rock the boat now? Why not just accept the unusual opportunity this weekend presented, and let it go at that?

All weekend he'd been free to do what he normally wouldn't, or couldn't. Not just kissing Piper, but holding her hand, as he had earlier today. As long as what they did here fell under the guise of pretending for the benefit of others, he could selfishly indulge in this time with her. Dancing, kissing, teasing, even sharing her family. But if it ever became something real, beyond this weekend, he'd lose her when they broke up.

The few women he hadn't dumped first had left him because he was too "emotionally inaccessible." And they were right. He'd been able to admit that, even as he hadn't really felt their loss. Until Dana. He'd really tried, dammit. He'd wanted to be what she needed, wanted to show her how he felt about her. But he'd learned too early in life not to make himself vulnerable to others to unlearn it now. Piper deserved a man who could love her unreservedly.

Too restless to stay in bed, he stood, absently registering the creaky groan of mattress springs at the shift in weight. He paced the small room. If his reluctance to commit was the only thing keeping them from a real chance at happiness, he might have a problem. But everything from their shared workplace to her celibate lifestyle meant friendship was the most logical relationship for them to have.

Yet logic didn't stop the way he'd felt when he'd watched her dance with Charlie. Logic couldn't ease the intense desire that rocked Josh each time he kissed her. And logic certainly hadn't helped him fall asleep hours ago instead of thinking about her all night long.

He pictured her in the blue skirt she'd worn earlier, her legs shapely and seductive beneath. In a baseball cap, jumping up and down and whooping victory at an Astros home game. Deep in concentration as she worked, oblivious to everything but the angles and lines of her drawings. In a mischievous mood, her aquamarine eyes sparkling like the ocean. In his arms...

Worse, she was in his heart. The truth he could no longer ignore was that he'd have to be an idiot not to want Piper.

But allowing himself to act on that would just mean more pain when it was over. Why let someone in when he'd still be alone in the end?

The words Piper had spoken blew through his mind like a cold, hostile wind. *"You give the illusion of going from one relationship to the next, but you don't let people get close to you, so you're actually more alone than I am."*

He was worried about being alone in the end?

"I'm alone now."

The truth dawned unpleasantly, shedding light into corners of his life he'd rather not examine. He'd told himself he lived a good life, and while that might be true in some ways, it was also a hollow life.

Piper could fill that hollowness.

Panic immediately radiated through him. Better to ignore the emptiness than risk their friendship. But... ignoring it wasn't working anymore.

Admittedly, the majority of his past relationships had been meaningless. He'd designed them that way so that no one would be hurt when either party walked away. But it was Piper who consumed his thoughts now, and his feelings for her, two years in the making, weren't shallow or easy. For the first time in his adult life, he couldn't just pick up and walk away. *So what do I do?*

Pursue a woman who scorned romantic attachments even while the thought of such an attachment still scared him?

Well, nothing else had worked. At least this way he could maybe follow up on those kisses they'd exchanged and ease the throbbing sexual need that had him so turned around he could barely think.

"Wow." Josh stood in the hall outside her hotel room, his wide eyes and gaping mouth making it clear that this wasn't his usual offhand flattery. He looked flummoxed.

Despite Piper's grim mood and the sleepless night she'd endured, she was happy to be responsible for the flummoxing. When she'd finally abandoned all hope of sleep and crawled out of bed a few hours ago, she'd decided she needed to look her best today. Falling in love with Josh was such a stupid thing to do that she'd needed some salve to her pride. A good hair day was about the best she could come up with on short notice.

In a pair of snug, dark green, cowgirl-cut jeans, which she'd only packed in a fit of nostalgia, and a high-collar shirt with a peekaboo cutout above her cleavage, she felt sexy in a uniquely Texan way. And with time to kill since she'd climbed out of bed so early, she'd curled her hair so that it spilled over her shoulders in soft waves. She'd even dabbed on some makeup.

Quite a change from the Piper of French braids and business suits. "The people at work would sure be surprised if I started showing up like this, wouldn't they?" Despite her words, Josh's was the only opinion she cared about.

He grinned down at her. "You go into the office looking like this, darlin', you won't get anything done with all the men hanging over your desk and drooling on your blueprints."

The exaggerated compliment actually deflated her. *He's just being Josh.* Still, as she turned to grab her purse from off the bed, she resolved to match his every teasing comment. No way would he ever guess that her heart was as cracked as a faulty foundation.

"Maybe I've been too focused on work, anyway," she drawled, walking toward him. She stepped outside the room and shut the door behind her before he had a chance to move back, forcing them to share personal space for just a second, bodies brushing. "There's something to be said for having a good time, don't you think?"

Too bad the man she wanted to have that good time with was so off-limits.

He swallowed. "Definitely. I'm all for a good time."

And not much else, she was afraid. Josh deserved so much more than the shallow relationships he allowed himself, but Piper couldn't force him to accept love he didn't want.

Subdued, she followed him down the carpeted hall. The plan was to grab a bite to eat from the continental breakfast buffet downstairs, then meet Blaine and Daphne near the town picnic grounds, where they'd return for the reunion after shopping. On the one hand, Piper looked forward to joining the other couple, since they could help alleviate some of the tension she felt around Josh. On the other hand, being around her happily married sister and brother-in-law would sting a little, too. Piper had always felt a twinge of pity for her sister, who'd never escaped Rebecca, but today she envied the love Daphne and her husband shared.

Today, Piper's pity was only for what she and Josh might have shared if circumstances were different.

PIPER STUDIED the wooded picnic area crowded with generations of Jamiesons and their families. A group of men were gathered around a cooler of cold beverages, while some younger members of the clan played Frisbee and catch. Still others sat at the tables, looking over photo albums and exchanging news. She was sure her name was being mentioned frequently. They were probably all still shocked that she'd attended, much less brought a man with her.

In retrospect, her lie hadn't been worth it. It would have been easier just to tell her mom she wasn't interested in dating than to deal with the confusion she felt now. Josh had been extra-attentive all day, his previous aversion to physical affection nowhere in evidence when he'd dropped his arm around her shoulders in the back seat of Blaine's car. When the four of them had been shopping, Josh hadn't come right out and said so, but she got the impression he wanted to be alone with her to talk about something. Although it was cowardly of her, she'd pretended to miss his signals, using Daphne's and Blaine's presence as a shield. Piper had meant what she'd told her sister—letting Josh know about her feelings was a *horrible* idea, the surest way to lose his friendship. Unfortunately, she wasn't sure how long she could conceal them if she was alone with him.

Walking next to her, Josh observed, "You have a really big family."

"Yep, my dad was the youngest of five kids." She looked up in time to catch the yearning in his eyes, and felt ashamed of all the times she'd griped about her relatives. She didn't need Josh to tell her that as a kid, he would've given anything for a family.

"Come on," she said gently, "I'll introduce you to everyone." They mixed and mingled among her cousins, then stopped for lemonade. As Piper turned to introduce him to more relatives, she was heralded by her great-aunt Millie.

"Piper!" Millie barreled forward, a determined expression on her wizened face. Not only did Millie always speak her mind, but, since she was mostly deaf, she usually spoke it loudly enough to be heard down the coast in Corpus Christi.

This afternoon was no different.

The thin, elderly woman stopped in front of Josh. "This must be your stud-muffin."

Piper tried to ignore the many heads that swiveled in their direction, as well as her great-aunt's unexpected—and somewhat disturbing—use of the term. "Josh, this is Great-Aunt Millie. Millie, Josh Weber."

He kissed Millie's hand, causing her to blush so becomingly that she looked years younger for a moment.

"Have you two set a date yet?"

"Uh, no," Piper said, "not yet."

"Well, don't dawdle," her great-aunt scolded. "A woman your age can't afford to wait. Only a few prime breeding years left." As though Piper were one of the heifers Millie and Great-Uncle Earl had once raised.

To avoid saying something she'd regret, Piper merely sipped her lemonade, wishing it were spiked.

Then Millie glanced at Josh and cackled. "But I'll bet you could still give her babies. A strapping young fellow like yourself is probably shooting more than blanks."

Piper choked, determined not to further commemorate the moment by shooting lemonade out her nose.

Millie shuffled off to terrorize other members of the Jamieson clan, and Piper apologized to Josh. "I swear that after this weekend you never have to see these people again."

"So you've said. Numerous times."

"Don't worry, I mean it."

He followed Millie's progress with his eyes. "The women in your family seem to get even more outspoken as they age." Grinning, he turned back to Piper. "Lord knows what you'll be like in forty or fifty years. Look out, world."

"Are you implying that I'm outspoken?"

"No, you're quiet and meek. And tall enough to be a supermodel, too." At her mock glare, he added, "Your not being a supermodel is a big loss to the men of the world. I don't know a woman sexier than you."

Oh, she wished he'd stop saying things like that. And she wished her imprudent heart wouldn't speed up when he did. "Josh, you're doing it again."

"Doing what?"

"When it's just you and me, you don't have to flirt."

"I've always flirted with you," he pointed out. "Long before this weekend. What's different now?"

Now I'm in love with you, and it hurts.

"Besides," he pressed, his expression growing alarmingly serious, "how do you know I *don't* find you sexy?"

"Because we're friends?" What was he trying to tell her? She knew from their kisses that he wasn't indifferent to her—she wasn't an idiot—but did he honestly want to act on the feelings growing between them?

"You think being your friend means I can't notice how funny and attractive and smart you are?" he challenged.

"Well..." Being friends certainly hadn't stopped her from noticing all those things about him. As she glanced away, trying to gather her thoughts, her gaze landed on a small, spry figure energetically winding up to pitch in the family softball game.

Nana? Yep, that was her grandmother—the very picture of health. In fact, as Piper watched her grandmother throw a fastball, she realized Nana looked to be in better shape than some of the much younger players on her team.

"I've been had." Piper practically growled the words. It had occurred to her that her mother might stretch the truth about Nana's condition, but to lie outright?

With Josh trailing after her, Piper stalked over to where Blaine and Daphne stood in the shade. "I want an answer. Are you people so desperate to get me married off that you let me believe someone I love was seriously ill?"

Blaine glanced guiltily to where Nana was in the process of striking out someone half her age. "Don't get mad at Daph. Nana *was* sick. It started out as just a cold, but when she developed some complications, she went to the hospital for observation. So when your mom said Nana had been ill, she wasn't lying. She just played it up because she knew you'd be more likely not to back out. And more likely to bring Josh for all of us to meet."

"I didn't know until just before you got here that Mom made the situation sound so dire," Daphne added hastily. "And Nana doesn't know at all."

"But that business about her not coming outside to meet me because she wasn't well?" Though definitely relieved about her grandmother's condition, Piper was plenty irritated.

"She's supposed to avoid the night air while she's still recovering from her respiratory infection," Daphne said. "Dad will drive her home early tonight so she doesn't catch a chill. Piper, you have every right to be annoyed with Mom. Just keep in mind that sometimes we lie to the people close to us, without even planning to, because we think it's what's best for them.''

Piper flushed at the subtle jab. How angry could she get with her mother for the deceptive exaggeration when Piper herself was guilty of comparable tactics? Maybe Daphne had been right last night about Piper and her mom having some traits in common. Besides, there was no point in staying mad at her mother when the universe was sure to pay Astrid back for the deception, anyway.

If Piper had learned one thing this weekend during her masquerade with Josh, it was that even the simplest white lies had a way of becoming complicated.

11

WHATEVER ELSE HAPPENED this weekend, Josh could honestly say he'd never been so well fed. Sitting at the picnic table, reflecting on the array of home-cooked food he'd enjoyed today, he knew he should feel mellow and full now, but mellow was difficult with Piper so close to him. Though he'd been trying—unsuccessfully—to get a few moments alone with her all day, her family's presence did have one current benefit. With everyone squished together on the bench, Piper was pressed into him from shoulder to thigh, her softness a tantalizing weight against him.

Her arm brushed his as she gestured during her conversation with Daphne, and his body hummed with awareness, like a generator kicking on, sending electricity to all the pertinent points. But this was nothing compared to a few moments ago, when Josh had reached past her and accidentally grazed her breast. They'd both frozen, and she'd stopped talking to her sister, turning to look into his eyes.

They were leaving tomorrow, and unless Josh seized the moment soon, he was going to lose his chance. The odds of their exploring the attraction between them, of finding out if they could be more than friends, were greater here. Once they returned to Houston, it would be too temptingly safe to fall back into their old routine, regardless of the passion he knew they invoked in each other.

"Hey." He tapped Piper on the shoulder, and she tilted her head back to look at him. "How about you and I go for a walk? Just the two of us," he added, lest she try to draft anyone else.

Seeing the uncertainty in her expression, he quickly appealed to the workout guilt she had to be feeling by now. "I figured we could burn off some of the calories we've been packing on all weekend."

"Well..." She frowned. "I guess we could."

They both stood, telling her immediate family that if they didn't see them later, they'd meet up with them in the morning for breakfast. Then they headed for one of the park's hiking paths, into the surrounding woods. The breeze carried the sounds of crickets chirping, owls hooting in the distance and armadillos scurrying in the underbrush.

"You were right," she told him, her brisk pace at odds with the cozy chat he'd been hoping to have. "I do need to burn off some calories."

"No, that was me trying to get you alone. Your body's perfect as is."

Her laugh was rueful. "Then you haven't been looking hard enough."

The hell he hadn't. "Tell you what. Strictly as a favor to you, I'm willing to make a more thorough evaluation. Clothing optional."

After a moment, she broke down and smiled, shaking her head. "Cute."

"I was hoping for 'irresistible,' but cute's a start."

"You know you're irresistible," she muttered.

Hope flashed as brightly as a shooting star. The very

fact that she sounded a bit ticked off made him think that her statement was more than an offhand remark. "You don't seem happy about it."

"Well, I...it's not important."

How she saw him was vitally important—high time he let her know that. But telling her the truth, even hinting at what the last few days had meant to him, what she'd come to mean to him... He took a deep breath, knowing that if he delayed much longer he'd fall back on the banter that was nothing more than a mask, and never take this chance.

"Piper, the last couple of days have been some of the best of my life."

She chuckled. "Oh, sure. With my mother practically measuring you for a tux, and me acting like I've developed multiple personality disorder—"

"Piper." He stopped walking, turning so that he stood in her path. "The last couple of days have been some of the best of my life." His tone brooked no argument, not even the playful kind, and she didn't respond. He took advantage of her rare speechlessness while he could. "Because of you. But don't get me wrong. In some ways, this weekend has been damn uncomfortable, too. Cold showers, for instance—zero fun. Plus, they're not much of a long-term solution."

"S-solution?"

"Yes." He bluntly stated what they'd danced around since their first night in Rebecca. "Our lusting after each other and not doing anything about it has definitely become a problem."

That had lacked the eloquence she deserved, but with the effect her nearness was having on him right now, he was lucky to be saying anything besides "you woman, me man." The way she was looking up at him, her lips softly parted, her eyes reflecting wonderment in the moonlight...

To hell with figuring out what to say to her. Who needed words? He gripped her shoulders with his hands and drew her closer, using less finesse than he normally managed, but Piper didn't object. She raised up on her toes to meet him, to kiss him for the first time with no witnesses. No excuses, no pretense, just their naked need for each other. His lips found hers, worshipping, ravishing, promising her a night she'd never forget.

His hands ran down the curve of her spine to cup the swell of her bottom, pulling her tighter against him, groaning at the friction of her body against his erection. No turning back now—they'd definitely passed the point of platonic. They just weren't as far past it as he'd like.

"Piper, if this isn't what you want, if you think we should stop—"

"No! I—I mean, I don't want to stop." She leaned back, looking around their wooded surroundings with wide eyes. "Delay, maybe. Can we go back to the hotel?"

Tiny lights exploded behind his eyes. Piper wanted to have sex with him! He was actually, finally, going to make love to her. Her ready acceptance left him speechless and feeling like the luckiest man alive. But, damn, he wished that hotel were closer.

He laced his fingers with hers. Though she walked with a quick stride, his legs were longer and he had to force himself not to drag her to the parking lot. They reached the car, but instead of unlocking the doors,

Josh pressed her up against the side, seeking her already upturned mouth.

A soft breathy sound escaped her, somewhere between a sigh and a moan. "Keys."

He fumbled in his pocket for the key ring, then handed them over to his favorite speedaholic. "You definitely drive. The less time this takes, the better."

Skirting around the front of the car, she shot him a wicked smile. "Then we're not thinking along the same lines."

He meant to laugh, but groaned instead, realizing just how much time he wanted to take exploring, tasting her body. If the drive to the hotel didn't kill him.

When he said as much, she chided, "Patience," but the urgency in her eyes was unmistakable and immensely gratifying.

"*Patience?* I've been waiting for this since the day I met you. It just took me awhile to realize it."

She shot him a look of such melting adoration that he wanted to reach across their seats and kiss her. She also hit the accelerator.

Piper didn't know what to say. His admission that he'd wanted her for so long took her breath away. She'd been fighting so fiercely to contain her desire for him, never believing she'd have a chance to act on her feelings, never thinking he'd let her that close.

At the hotel, she slammed the car into Park, and he rushed out to open her door for her. After they'd hurried up the stairs like impatient newlyweds, he unlocked the door to his room and swept her into his arms, carrying her inside. She felt like a bride going over the threshold, but the matrimonial analogy didn't bother her as it once might have. In fact, she experienced a twinge of wistfulness, but it was quickly replaced by the heady sensation of being in Josh's arms.

Fumbling one-handed with the small lamp on the nightstand, he set her down beside his bed, his mouth already on hers before her feet touched the floor. The deft way he kissed her, like a man who knew all her secrets, sent desire spiraling through her. His hands were at her waist, pressing her against him, and she mentally cursed the layers of clothing separating them. She smiled inwardly, though, at the chance to finally unbutton his shirt and slide it off his shoulders. When she'd dreamed of doing this, she hadn't realized her hands would be shaking.

She laid a palm across his bare chest, tracing her fingers over the smattering of hair and the muscles toned from recreational weight lifting. "I've imagined this, you know."

"Really?" He sounded pleased that she'd pictured being with him, but then he laughed. "Please tell me your fantasy didn't stop here."

Their kiss muffled her answering laugh. She explored his mouth, then slowly lowered herself from her tiptoes to kiss his jaw and run her tongue over his collarbone. Her fingers went to the waistband of his jeans, but he lightly encircled her wrist, stopping her.

"Wait. I want to see you." He met her eyes, his gaze hypnotically sensual, as he released each button on her shirt with much more dexterity than she'd exhibited. "You're not the only one who's thought about this."

Cool air hit her skin as he pushed the material of her shirt away, but the appreciative gleam in his eyes more than kept her warm. He skimmed his fingers along her rib cage, trailing upward, seemingly in no hurry, though his breathing grew more labored. He cupped her breasts, his fingers grazing their already stiff peaks through the lace of her bra. A spasm of need went through her midsection, leaving her light-headed.

Tugging gently at his hand, she sat on the bed before her legs gave out beneath her. Josh followed, kissing her again, building the waves of feeling inside her until she thought she'd drown. The possibility of losing herself in the undertow was exciting rather than frightening. She sank back against the mattress, pulling him with her, wanting his weight above her.

When he broke off their kiss to remove her bra, she moaned in protest, but it quickly turned to a sound of approval as he bent his head and took one hardened nipple between his lips. He turned his attention to her other breast, and Piper gripped his hips with her hands, undulating her body against his in an instinctive attempt to assuage the slow burn she felt.

Again her fingers went to the waistband of his jeans. He made no move to stop her this time as she lowered the zipper with some effort, her task made more difficult by his blatant arousal. She tugged the jeans and briefs down together, her eyes widening at his impressive erection. Knowing how much he wanted her gave her an electric rush, filling her with a tingling, ultra-feminine satisfaction. She curved her fingers around him, sliding over the smooth rigid length.

His breath hitched. "You're amazing."

Piper couldn't find her voice, but she silently returned the sentiment. She'd never experienced this before. Not the fiery driving physical sensations and not the maelstrom of emotions, either. Happy and nervous and calm all at once. Nothing had ever felt more right.

Moving together, they fumbled with her remaining clothes, and she wriggled free of them, desperately needing to be flesh-to-flesh. He traced one strong, lightly callused hand down over her abdomen and between her thighs, resting the heel of his palm on her. The contact, slight and unmoving, teased her senses. Tense with a sweet pain only Josh could ease, she moved against him, seeking more. His response was to scoot down the bed, replacing his hand with his mouth, kissing her intimately.

Unused to feeling so vulnerable to another person, exposed in a way not even being naked could approach, Piper stiffened at first. But she'd already given Josh her heart. She wanted to give him her body now. She relaxed, surrendering herself to the man she loved and the dizzying heat of desire. His tongue moved on her, and her involuntary sounds of need mingled with the pounding of her own heartbeat in her ears. Soon her entire body pulsed with that rhythm. She climaxed in spasms that left her clinging to his shoulders, somehow utterly replete and yet feeling empty, wanting him to fill her and complete what they'd started together.

He moved away only long enough to deal with a condom, then aligned his body with hers. When he entered her, the oxygen left her lungs in a whoosh, but she didn't need air. Only Josh.

And he gave himself to her, as generously and thoroughly as she ever could have imagined. Over and over, until the swells of passion crashed through her, propelling her forward into a second orgasm. Her body clenched, drawing him even more tightly into her. Glancing up, she watched his face, taut with desire, as he found his own release.

They held each other, their ragged breathing and thundering hearts the only sounds in the small room. Piper wasn't sure she'd ever be able to think or speak coherently again, so she was glad that it took Josh at least a few minutes to regain his composure, as well.

Rolling slightly to the side, he leaned close, framing her face with his hands, pushing back slightly damp strands of hair. "That was incredible."

Instead of giving her a chance to find her voice, he kissed her. Perhaps that was for the best, because the only thing she could think of to say right now was "I love you."

So say it, she told herself later, when they both lay on their sides and Josh had his arm around her. She snuggled against him, enjoying the way he idly traced one hand up and down her back. But not even the closeness of the moment gave her quite enough courage to bluntly state her feelings. It was such an irrevocable admission, and not knowing how he would respond ate at the edges of her perfect contentment.

Josh's breathing eventually deepened, and she realized he'd fallen asleep. She envied his relaxed slumber. Moments ago, she'd felt weightless and carefree. Now she worried that even after knowing him for two years, and the intimacy they'd just shared, she still couldn't guess what his reaction to her feelings would be. No question that he saw her as more than a platonic friend...but how much more? Perhaps she should have thought to ask these questions earlier, but thinking had been the last thing she'd wanted to do.

As her intoxicating afterglow faded, Piper realized

there was a lot she didn't know. Such as what they were going to do about their relationship once they got back to Houston and a shared office where they weren't supposed to *have* a relationship? And would Josh even consider this a relationship?

She grimaced at the tension slowly knotting her muscles. She would have thought her sated body would stay relaxed and boneless a little longer. After all, she'd just had the best sex of her life.

She only hoped great sex wasn't all it had been.

12

JOSH STIFLED A YAWN, the conversation around the Jamiesons' dining room table momentarily receding to a dull buzz. After breakfast, he and Piper were headed back to Houston, and for once he wouldn't mind if she wanted to drive. Considering all his missed sleep last night, he'd be happy to doze in the passenger seat on the return trip.

Around two in the morning, he'd awakened from a dream about Piper to the reality of Piper. The naked, warm satiny reality. He'd brushed aside her citrus-scented hair and kissed the back of her neck, still drowsy enough that his intentions weren't truly carnal. But then she'd stirred, moving her softly curved bottom against the one part of him that was fully awake. They'd ended up making love a second time, teasing and exploring each other almost in slow motion, with the kind of delicious languor that made the interlude seem more fantasy than reality once morning broke.

Except that fantasies didn't rob him of his sleep. Or leave a tiny bruised love bite above Piper's collarbone that had forced her to change shirts twice this morning so her family wouldn't see it. Though the mark had been unintentional, Josh couldn't help taking a small amount of satisfaction in the physical proof that Piper was...

What? His? Piper would never belong *to* any man, so

the most a guy could hope for was to make her see that she belonged *with* him. Josh frowned inwardly, absently pouring syrup into a thick, sticky puddle over a homemade Belgian waffle, wondering how Piper viewed last night. This morning, they'd overslept and had rushed through getting ready so they could check out of the hotel and be on time for breakfast. He'd kissed her and she'd kissed him back, but they hadn't talked. He supposed they could have in the car on the way to her parents, but neither of them had mentioned it.

Just as well. Josh didn't know what to say.

Last night had certainly shown him the rewards for letting someone into his life. He couldn't remember ever being as happy as he'd been. But he did remember the last two times he'd dared hope for true happiness—the day the Wakefields had told him they'd be adopting him and the day he'd told Dana he loved her.

"Josh?" Mrs. Jamieson's worried voice seemed to be coming from far away, and he blinked to bring her into focus. "You okay? You seem exhausted this morning."

His gaze slid involuntarily to Piper, who guiltily stifled a yawn of her own as her mother spoke.

He grinned, his mood improved by Piper's sleepy expression. "I'm fine, ma'am. Just thinking that the weekend went by too fast."

"You can come back soon for the wedding, though," Blaine said. "I'm tired of being the only guy for Piper and Daphne to abuse verbally. This way, we're evenly matched."

"Two women pitting wits against two guys isn't an even match," Josh said with a chuckle. "We'll get slaughtered." But his joking was forced. Would he see any of Piper's family again?

An hour later, breakfast was finished, the dishes were in the kitchen and the Jamiesons had trooped outside to bid Piper and Josh farewell.

Piper hugged Daphne goodbye, and Josh couldn't help noticing a new easiness between the two sisters, an affection that was more relaxed than it had been when he and Piper arrived. The weekend in Rebecca seemed to have helped her work a few things out.

"I wish I could be here when the twins are born," Piper said.

"Me, too," Daphne agreed. "But a due date is as far from a sure thing as a lottery ticket. You could always drive down when I go into labor, but I don't really want you trying to make the trip between Houston and Rebecca at three in the morning."

Piper laughed. "Well, maybe you'll be one of those women no one ever hears about, one who goes into labor at a respectable hour, like 9:00 a.m., instead of the middle of the night. And if not...I'll just have to come home for Christmas and spend time with you and my new nephews then."

For a moment, silence reigned, then her family all began talking at once.

"You make sure to bring Josh with you," Nana instructed, so commanding that he wondered how he or Piper ever could have believed she was frail. "I'm so glad you finally found a good man to take care of you."

"Honey, you're welcome here anytime," Mrs. Jamieson assured her daughter. "Whether you have a boyfriend with you or not. We don't care."

Piper did a double take. "You don't?"

"No." Her mother shot Josh an apologetic look. "Not that we wouldn't be thrilled to have you over for Christmas, of course."

"What about all those lectures?" Piper demanded. "The ones about how I wasn't getting any younger? The pressure to marry Charlie?"

Mrs. Jamieson winced. "I've realized this weekend how much I love having you visit...and how much I've driven you away. I didn't mean to put so much pressure on you, it's just that marrying your father and having you and Daphne made me so happy. I wanted you to be that happy."

"Even if what makes me happy is work and friends, not a relationship?"

Mrs. Jamieson glanced from Piper to Josh. "Well, sure, honey. But you have found a great relationship."

"Right," Piper agreed quickly. "It was more a hypothetical question."

"A moot point is what it is, " Nana said. "You and Josh will be here in December. I'll get started on his Christmas quilt."

"Quilt?" Josh parroted.

Piper glanced over her shoulder. "Jamieson tradition."

And Nana wanted to include him in the family custom? The dangerous longing he'd been suppressing since he was sixteen welled within him—the desire to belong.

They aren't your family. They include you because of Piper, and you don't even know if the two of you have a future. The dark voice in his head was one he knew well, the same one that had talked him out of hope before.

Not a cheerful voice, granted, but it had saved him from further pain and disappointment.

Today the voice seemed darker than ever, and Josh was torn. He wanted to change, he really did. He wanted to be sure of his feelings for Piper and hers for him, wanted to hope for the best. Despite parents being killed, foster families getting transferred to Europe, girlfriends walking out because of his inability to connect, happy endings *did* happen sometimes, right? It worked out for some people.

For some people, maybe, the voice conceded. *But for you?*

BY THE TIME PIPER LOOKED through the windshield and saw the Houston City Limits sign, she'd reached an unpleasant but inescapable realization: she was a big fat coward. Okay, given the strict gym schedule she subjected herself to, maybe the fat part wasn't necessary. But she'd definitely shown a lack of courage during their drive from Rebecca back to the city. Why hadn't she said anything to Josh about last night?

Because it was difficult to express what last night meant to her when she had no idea what it might have meant to him. She supposed she could ask about his innermost feelings and thoughts. Yeah, because that strategy had always worked really well for women in his past.

"We're almost there." She didn't even want to think about how inane she sounded—pointing out that he was about five minutes from his own home in case he'd somehow missed that—but she'd needed something, anything, to temporarily slice through the silence of everything they weren't saying.

Josh nodded, but didn't pry his gaze from the window he'd been staring out of for the past few hours. First, he'd shown an inexplicable fascination with watching miles of pastureland and the occasional cow. The bucolic landscape had given way to the slithering freeways and overpasses of Houston. Now he stared unblinkingly at the coppery reflection of the setting sun across the buildings of the city skyline.

Despite the awkward way time was dragging inside the car, Piper still felt that they were nearing their apartment complex much too soon. One more street to go, then their weekend would officially be over. Surely they weren't just going to have sex after two years of platonic friendship, then ignore it. Was she supposed to pretend that nothing had happened, hop out of the car, hand Josh his luggage and tell him goodbye?

Don't be melodramatic. The man works with you and lives one story above you. It's hardly goodbye.

So what was it, then?

"Josh—" *We need to talk.* She stopped herself just in time from uttering the dreaded phrase. Gee, maybe if she thought really hard she could come up with something even more trite to say that would send him hurling himself from a moving vehicle even faster.

Something in her tone must have penetrated the invisible wall of self-isolation he'd been projecting all day, because he turned to briefly meet her gaze. "Is this about last night?"

She tried not to ponder how many times he may have had about-last-night conversations with other women—or how those conversations had ended. "Yes."

"I'm sorry, Piper."

The pit of her stomach began sinking like the post-iceberg *Titanic.* "You're sorry we made love?"

"No! I'm not sorry we— I was apologizing for the awkwardness today, not what happened last night. I didn't know what to say, so I thought I'd take the easy way out and just take my cue from you."

Her laugh bordered more on a nervous giggle. "Figures. The one time I decide to follow a man's lead." She steered her car into the parking garage.

"Can I help you carry in your stuff," Josh offered, "or would that offend your feminist sensibilities?"

"Maybe I can make an exception just this once."

After she parked the car, they divided the bags and rode the elevator up together. She unlocked her front door, and Josh followed her inside, setting down her stuff and shifting his own luggage from one hand to the other.

"I hate to not eat and run, but I should get upstairs," he said. "Unpack, check messages, get my laundry done before work tomorrow."

"Yeah, I should do all that, too." Doing everyday tasks seemed surreal—how could she just go about her normal, mundane tasks when so much had changed for her this weekend? "Well...thanks for everything."

"My pleasure." The perfect opportunity for an outrageous comment or at least a wicked gleam in his eye to give his words double-entendre emphasis, but Josh simply rocked back on his heels.

They stood in awkward silence, him like a bellhop waiting for a tip and her like a hotel guest who just realized she didn't have any cash on her.

He turned toward the open door, but then paused. "Piper, have dinner with me tomorrow night."

Her heart fluttered. "Dinner?"

"Yeah. A real dinner date, not just a shared pizza at Grazzio's."

Thank God. Piper breathed a sigh of relief. What they'd shared had been more than a weekend fling out of town. She just had to be patient. Even if Josh felt the same way she did, he would probably be more skittish about expressing it. The man's entire life had been people leaving him. Wouldn't the best way to encourage him to change be to demonstrate she was willing to modify her ways, too?

And she did mean *modify*—a willing compromise that she'd thought of herself, not a complete reinvention to satisfy another person. She'd learned something this weekend, and although her relationship with Charlie had taken an unhealthy turn, doing something for someone you cared about did not make you a spineless throwback to the fifties.

She wanted to show Josh she was giving this her all, make some sort of gesture. "Dinner sounds great. But instead of going out, what if I cook here?"

For a moment, he looked stunned, then his gold-green eyes glinted with amusement. "Want me all to yourself?"

She grinned. "Come over tomorrow and find out. Just let me know what time works for you. I'd planned to stay a little late at the office to catch up, but—" Good grief. The office. How had she forgotten? "What are we going to do about work?"

The humor in his gaze disappeared, like a light going out, leaving his expression dark and carefully blank. "You mean the no-dating policy?"

"Yeah."

"No need to decide that right this second, is there?" He was trying to sound nonchalant, but his tone was as guarded as his features. "We keep everything to ourselves for now, and if this develops into anything, we'll figure out what to do later."

If it develops? Didn't they at least rate as "something," already? Nice to see they were both giving this their all.

"Piper, maybe that didn't come out right."

"No, it's okay. I know what you meant." She used her best worldly, unhurt, I'm-a-big-girl tone.

"Do you? Because you look upset. I didn't mean that this *wasn't* anything, only that..." He shoved his hands into his pockets. "Men just aren't good with words."

You are when you're trying to seduce women. It was only after the seduction had been accomplished that the charmers didn't know what to say.

JOSH WAS SO HAPPY to see Piper Monday night that it startled him. After all, they'd been in the same office all day. But he hadn't said two words to her there. He didn't waste time with words once she opened the door to her apartment, either.

Instead, he lowered his free hand—the one not holding the bottle of wine—to her waist and pulled her to him for a kiss hello. His greeting apparently took her by surprise, because at first she was simply soft and pliant beneath his mouth. Then she brushed her tongue against his, kissing him back with enough heat that he almost dropped the merlot.

In what seemed like the far distance, the elevator beeped, signaling that the doors were about to part.

Josh realized that he and Piper should probably step into her apartment before they took this any further.

He pulled away reluctantly, smiling down at her. "You look great." She'd come to work today dressed as a hybrid of Houston Piper and Rebecca Piper. Neither braiding her hair back nor letting it fall completely free, she'd instead pulled the sides up with delicate barrettes. She'd also skipped the usual pantsuit in favor of a sweater in muted reds and yellows, over a long black skirt. "I've been wanting to tell you that all day, but I figured I'd save the hitting on you until after work."

She grinned. "Better late than never."

Following her inside, he thought to himself that he might have been the only one on the drafting floor who hadn't hit on her today. Even Smith had lingered near her workstation after they'd finished discussing some specs on a new building. Josh had itched to storm over there and stake his claim, but of course he hadn't.

Quite the opposite. He'd stayed as far away from Piper as possible. Now more than ever, it was important to keep up a professional appearance. His reward for keeping a businesslike distance was enjoying her company tonight.

He trailed her into the galley-style kitchen and set the wine on the pale green counter. "I hope red is okay, I wasn't sure what we were having."

"Lasagna sound good?"

"Sounds great." Not that he was here for the food. "Anything I can do to help?"

She picked up a small container of cottage cheese and emptied it into a white plastic bowl, cocking her head toward the refrigerator. "You can make a salad, if you like. I hit the grocery store on the way home, so there are actual vegetables in there that were grown during our lifetime.''

"If it's green, grab it and chop it up. If it's fuzzy and black, pretend I didn't see it. Got it.''

She shot a mock glare over her shoulder before turning back to the bowl. She added ricotta and blended the contents with an electric mixer. Josh found the salad ingredients, taking them and a small wooden cutting board over to the corner apartment management generously designated "the breakfast nook." He sat at the table chopping, but couldn't help glancing in Piper's direction every couple of seconds, despite the danger to his fingers.

God, she's beautiful. Just looking at her made him ache inside. The fact that he'd pushed for this dinner gave him hope, because the truth was, when they'd arrived back in Houston, he'd wanted to run like hell. Away from her and away from the emotional devastation she'd wreak when she left.

If. If she left, he tried to tell himself.

Piper finished layering pasta, meat sauce and cheese in a pan and placed the lasagna in the oven. Then she pulled out two glasses and a corkscrew.

"How about some of that wine now?" she asked, opening the bottle.

He carried the salad into the kitchen. "Sure." He started to pour some of the merlot into a glass for her, but almost spilled it when she leaned forward to rest her arms on the countertop. Obviously she didn't realize that he could see straight down her loose sweater.

Or—he noticed the sly, secretive curve of her lips— maybe she knew exactly what she was doing. He stole a second glance at the lacy black bra she wore. Piper was just full of surprises tonight.

She straightened, sipping her wine. "Missed you at work today."

"I was there." He tried joking it off. "I was the guy you couldn't see from behind the overflowing pile in my In box."

"I guess so. I mean, I know it's my fault you're backed up, but maybe we can have lunch together sometime this week."

He drank his wine, stalling. The last thing he wanted to discuss was their work week. He'd told Piper last night that there was no reason to figure out a way around the no-dating policy just yet, but she was too forthright a woman to accept deception as a long-term solution. Josh couldn't wrap his mind around the alternatives.

Would Piper quit her job because of a man? No chance in hell. And when he considered quitting...it was such a drastic move. Too permanent for a guy like him. He couldn't alter his life like that without knowing for sure that the person he was doing it for would be around for the long haul. And how could he ever be sure?

"Josh. Did I lose you?"

"Sorry. I got preoccupied by this incredibly sexy woman."

"Oh." She smiled up at him, flirting from beneath her lashes. "You're forgiven."

"You're no fun at all." He set his wineglass on the counter and reached out to take hers from her hand. "I had very specific plans for how I was going to earn your forgiveness."

The delicate pulse in the hollow of her throat quickened. "I take it back, then. You're not forgiven. I predict it's going to take considerable work on your part to appease me."

He leaned in without yet touching her, letting the anticipation build for both of them. "Guess I'd better get started then."

She stretched up to reach him. Josh lowered his head, but then stopped.

"Wait. I have a better idea." He turned and lifted her so she was sitting on the edge of the counter, solving their height difference.

Her lips met his in a deep, openmouthed kiss, rich with the heady flavor of the wine. He braced one hand on the countertop next to her and cupped the other behind her head, his fingers tangled in the silk of her hair. Josh kissed her like a man experiencing water for the first time after days lost in the desert. He wanted to drink in everything about her—her sweet taste, each breathy sigh and sensuous movement.

Dropping his hands behind her, he lifted the hem of her sweater and ran his fingers over her bare back, tracing her spine. She quivered beneath his touch, and he continued to kiss her as he slid his hands around to her flat abdomen. He slowly worked his way up to the lace cups of her bra.

He traced his thumb over one pebbled nipple, and she kissed him with growing ardor, meeting the thrust of his tongue. He felt her hands at the front of his shirt and smiled against her mouth when he realized she'd popped one of the buttons off in her zeal to get him out of his clothes.

Luckily, he had no buttons to contend with. All he

had to do was draw back for the ten seconds it took to whisk the autumn-colored sweater over her head. She sat on the counter, a temptress in her unlikely attire of barely-there black bra and long black skirt that revealed nothing yet seduced the imagination.

"That's a good look for you," he said, his husky tone probably a truer indication of his desire than the compliment.

Running a hand over his chest, she lightly raked her fingernails against his skin. "Is this still part of your apology for not listening? If so, feel free to tune out as often as you'd like."

Under other circumstances, he might have laughed, but at the moment he was too aroused. Piper dropped her hands to his waist, slipping her fingers through the belt loops of his pants, tugging him closer. Then she moved to the zipper, lowering it millimeter by millimeter, leaving him hard and aching for her touch.

Josh stepped out of his pants, kicking them across her tile floor. She scooted closer to the edge of the counter, trying to press her body to his. A whimper of frustration escaped her when the narrow skirt got in her way. He bunched up the fabric, caressing the satiny skin of her thighs as he did so, and stood between her legs.

The tiny black lace panties she wore nearly sent him over the edge. It wasn't just the lingerie that affected him, or even the surprise of finding them on a woman who normally didn't indulge in lacy, feminine clothes. The real turn-on was how well he understood her, how right he'd been about her. He'd realized months ago that beneath the genderless pantsuits and supposed disinterest in sex existed a fiercely passionate woman, a woman Piper didn't let others see. But she'd chosen to reveal that side of herself to him.

"Nice," he told her, tracing the lacy edges of the panties, brushing his hand over the short curls concealed underneath. "But I hope you don't mind if I take them off."

She wiggled her hips to accommodate him. "If you insist. But the panties and the bra are really a matching set...."

"I see what you mean." He reached up to flick open the delicate front clasp, filling his hands with her.

She was so perfect, so responsive. He stroked one nipple, watching her face as he rolled the bud between his fingers. When she arched her back and offered herself up to him, he lowered his head to her breasts, paying lavish homage with his mouth

"Did you want to move this to your bedroom?" Because if she did, they should head that direction *now*.

She locked her legs around his waist, as though trying to prevent him from going anywhere. As if there was anyplace he'd rather be. "No. Here."

The sexy rasp of need in her voice made him almost lose it right there. He grabbed a condom from his pants pocket and started to put it on. Brushing his hand away, she unrolled the latex over him slowly, squeezing just hard enough with her fingers for his breath to catch.

Grasping her hips, he sheathed himself inside her. Piper pulled back slightly, angling her body so that he slid in deeper. Her gaze met his, her eyes filled with love and rapture he couldn't believe he deserved. Couldn't believe would last. He'd never felt so connected to anyone, and the intensity overwhelmed him.

Emotions he never let himself feel rushed at him, and, for a fraction of a second, panic eclipsed the ecstasy of being inside her.

He closed his eyes, trying to find a safe distance. He wanted to ignore the emotion and the risk it represented, and lose himself in their physical connection, use the incredible sensations to shut out his fear and pretend that his heart wasn't hers for the breaking. Wordlessly apologizing to her with his body, he made love to her with slow smooth strokes that took all of his self-control and wrung pleasure-drenched moans from her.

She gasped. "That is s-so good."

He rocked his hips, Piper hot and tight around him. "You mean right...there?"

"Mmm, yes. *Right* there."

Another motion of his hips caused another soft gasp, this one slightly louder and more ragged. Wanting to make this perfect for her, wanting to atone for that piece of himself he was deliberately withholding, he moved inside her, holding back until her nails dug into his skin. She shattered around him, her muscles working to push him to his own shuddering release.

Her head rested against his chest, her body rising and falling as she tried to catch her breath. He hugged her to him, his own breathing too labored for him to form words. Even if he'd been able to speak, he knew he wouldn't voice the thought screaming in his head: *I love you.*

He hadn't said it in years—not since he'd forced himself to tell Dana as she was leaving. But it had been too little, too late, and she hadn't even turned to acknowledge the stricken admission. She'd simply walked out the door, out of his life, and he'd sworn then and there never to be hurt like that again.

It wasn't the memory that hurt so much as the realization that his love for Piper was harder won and ran much deeper. The pain of losing her would be excruciating. So he choked on the words he knew she deserved to hear.

13

FOUR DAYS LATER they'd made love in Piper's kitchen, her shower and, just now, rather athletically, on the floor of her living room. They'd made love in her bed last night, after already having sex bent over her desk, but Josh hadn't been able to sleep. And she hadn't complained when he'd awakened her.

Now he tilted his head back from his seated position on the floor, sprawled against the base of the sofa. Piper sat above him on the couch, wearing his shirt. "You know, we should really try to make it to the bed more often," he stated.

"I know what you mean." She leaned down to kiss him, laughter in her voice. "I think I have rug burn...but it was worth it."

The sex had been incredible—when wasn't it?—but it was the only time he felt at peace, able to push his doubts away. In the week since they'd returned from Rebecca, he'd had some of the most intensely wonderful moments he'd ever experienced. But also some of the scariest, and the anxiety was wearing on him. Josh lived in a constant state of waiting for the other shoe to drop.

Today, he'd tried to prove something to himself. He'd survived plenty of other goodbyes in his life, and if he and Piper ever parted ways, he could survive that, too. To illustrate the point, he'd avoided her all day, told himself that it wouldn't kill him to go without talking to her, touching her. He could be fine without her.

He'd noticed her questioning glances at work, but she hadn't approached him. She'd given him his space, which had made staying away that much more difficult. He'd tried to appease his conscience, and his need to reach out to her, by sending her an e-mail that said he was swamped and would be staying late, but would love to see her over the weekend.

Then he'd blown the whole thing by knocking on her front door an hour ago and asking if she wanted to watch the last half of a football game with him. Clearly, his little "self demonstration" had been a complete failure.

He reached up now, running his hand over the smooth muscle of her calf. "I'm sorry I...was so busy today."

"No problem." But her smile didn't reach her eyes, and she quickly looked away, glancing at the ignored television set, where football had been replaced by a syndicated sitcom. "Sorry you didn't get to see any of the game."

"Really?"

This time the smile was genuine. "No. Not really. Given the same situation, I'd seduce you all over again. Besides, football's not my thing. Just a way to kill time until baseball season."

Next spring. Thinking that far into the future caused a dizzying nausea.

She entwined one arm around his neck and tousled his hair with her other hand. "Hey, if you'd like to give that bed thing another shot—"

"As tempting as that sounds, I can't stay." Holding her last night should have been bliss. Instead it had been hours of tossing and turning and second-guessing. Besides, he shouldn't have come down here tonight at all.

"Oh. You're going?"

He could tell by her tone that she was hurt, and annoyance crept into his voice—only she wasn't the one with whom he was annoyed. "I stayed last night."

"I know. I just…"

"I'm still way behind. My sideline stuff doesn't magically take care of itself."

She rose from the sofa. "There's no reason to get condescending. Hold on. I'll go change so you can have your shirt back."

Regret bubbled up in him. "I don't have to leave this second."

"No, you should. The sooner you tackle that work, the sooner you'll get caught up." But her blue-green eyes said she wanted him gone. He'd hurt her, and she was ready for him to be on his way.

"Unless your plan isn't to get caught up," she muttered as she walked toward her bedroom.

"What's that supposed to mean?"

She paused at the doorway, turning to glare at him. "You think I haven't noticed how busy you suddenly are at work?"

"I've always been busy at work. So have you."

"Exactly. And yet we've still had time to talk for a minute in the break room or grab lunch together. You've been ignoring me, Josh."

The knot of fear in his chest tightened. Four days, and she was already unhappy. Fragments of conversations with Dana came back to him: *"I can't reach you, Josh...I need someone who's really there for me..."* Had it started so soon?

"What about this? Just now?" He spread his arms to encompass her living room, where items of clothing were still strewn about.

"You mean dropping by to have sex? Isn't that what's referred to as a booty call?"

The disdain in her voice sliced through him, and he felt cornered. "I didn't hear you complaining a few minutes ago."

She opened her mouth, but then stopped, holding up a hand. "You know what? Let's not do this. It's been a long day, and we were both busy. I'm glad you came by, Josh, I am. And I don't want to fight."

"Me, neither. Piper—"

Shaking her head, she interrupted, "Just give me a second to change. It's okay." But she didn't turn away quickly enough to hide the bright sheen of unshed tears.

And he couldn't help noticing that, even though they'd spent most of their time this week naked together, when she went into her room to change, she firmly closed the door behind her.

I'VE HAD IT. Piper stomped into the gym locker room the following Wednesday morning, knowing that she had to talk to someone or she was going to lose her mind. She hung her work clothes from the hook inside her locker, then slammed the door hard enough that the resulting metallic clang reverberated throughout the room.

She'd seen Gina last week, but for some reason

hadn't shared any of the details of what had happened between her and Josh. Instead, she'd simply told her friend that she'd reached a new understanding with her family and would probably be seeing them again at Christmas. At the time, Piper had made excuses for her silence, such as it would be embarrassing to tell Gina that she and Josh were having a red-hot affair after all the times she'd insisted they were just friends, or the relationship was so new that she was savoring it before telling her friends. But the truth she could no longer escape was that she hadn't told Gina anything about Josh last week because, deep down, Piper knew things were wrong between them.

On the surface, the situation looked pretty good. In Rebecca, she had concluded that she loved the man and wanted more than platonic friendship. They'd taken their relationship to a new level, and had been spending a lot of their free time having phenomenal sex. Although twice now he'd left shortly after the phenomenal sex.

Where was the problem? She'd never been clingy, and she wasn't about to start now. She wasn't the type of woman who *had* to have a man stay over. But she couldn't ignore her gut feeling that Josh was the type of man who had to leave. In reality, while their lovemaking might be the stuff of erotic legend, she didn't want a legend. She wanted her friend back.

It was an odd paradox, but the closer they got physically, the more she felt she was losing him emotionally. It seemed as though they barely talked, and she missed that. She supposed she could have passed on the sex at any given time, but she wanted it as much as he did. She just wanted more with it. Was she being too greedy? Too hypersensitive? She needed a second opinion.

Ready to talk to Gina about the problem, Piper left the locker room, hoping her friend was already upstairs. She took the carpeted steps two at a time, the loud, familiar cadence of weight machines in use not as soothing today as she normally found it. Though the main workout floor was hardly deserted, there weren't enough people that Piper had trouble spotting her friend. Eye-catching in a bright red *I Object* T-shirt, Gina stood near the water fountain smiling at a dark-haired man who looked as if he was trying his best to overcome any objections she might have.

A pang of guilt jabbed Piper. Though not intentionally condescending, she had never understood Gina's yearning to find someone. Now she did. Piper had been saying for months that she was content with her life—her job, her family, her friends—but she'd realized that she wanted more than contentment. She wanted passion and laughter, someone who could share her triumphs and defeats.

No, not just "someone." She wanted Josh. She didn't know who Gina wanted, but Piper hoped her friend found him.

Gina glanced up with an acknowledging smile as Piper approached. "Hey, lady."

"Hey." When her friend's dark-haired admirer returned to his workout, Piper added, "Am I glad to see you this morning. If you don't mind listening, I could use a friendly ear."

"Don't mind at all. Makes it worth my showing up. I almost slept in this morning. Some days I just can't get excited about the thought of hitting the treadmill."

Suddenly Piper felt exactly the same way. She'd told herself that maybe exercise would help clear her mind, but that was ridiculous. She and Josh had already shared enough aerobic activity this week to elevate her to a Zenlike state of clarity.

"What if we ditch our normal disciplined routine?" Piper suggested rebelliously. "Let's get out of here, and I'll buy you a doughnut."

"Doughnuts over discipline?" For a moment, Gina seemed as though she might lay her palm against Piper's forehead to check for fever and delirium. "Since when do *you* do what's tempting instead of sensible?"

Piper bit her lip. "Funny you should ask."

"I CAN'T BELIEVE IT." It was probably the eighth time Gina had restated that sentiment since Piper had filled her in, but who was counting? "I really can't believe you did it."

"Yeah, I'm sensing that." Piper leaned back in her U-shaped, overstuffed chair, thinking that the furniture in the coffeehouse might be even more comfortable than what she had at home. "Just let me know when you get past the whole Josh-and-Piper-slept-together part, so we can figure out what I should do."

"I might never get past that part!" Gina brushed powdered sugar off her hands, still shaking her head in disbelief. "Do you know how many times you lectured me about you and Josh just being friends?"

"I didn't lecture, exactly." People who'd never met Piper's mom had no idea what a lecture was. "Besides, we really *were* just friends. But that, um, changed over the weekend." Into what, she didn't know.

"At least now I understand why you refused to set me up with the guy."

"No, that's not—" Piper broke off, realizing Gina was kidding. Mostly. "All right. I get it. You told me so. I've been denying the truth to myself and everyone else, yada yada. You were right, I was wrong. But now what?"

Gina's smirk faded into a more empathetic expression. "You feel like he's using you for sex?"

No, that wasn't it.

Was it?

"It's more that I feel like...when we're not having sex, he's shutting me out. But I don't know how to say anything to him without sounding like one of those needy women whining about how she wants more attention. Especially when I think he's trying. Considering Josh's track record, this could be the most serious relationship he's ever had. But that track record makes me nervous. I half expect to come home to a note on my door telling me he's joined the French Foreign Legion or something."

"You think he'll find an excuse to leave."

He had with every woman before her. Piper would love to think she was different, special, but had he given her any real reason to believe this would last? And did she even want it to last if she couldn't have Josh both as her friend and as her lover?

"I never considered myself insecure," She said, "but how can I feel good about this when we're actually less close than we were before?" She lowered her voice just in case the background sounds of chatting customers, percolating coffee and rustling newspapers weren't enough to blot out the finer points of her sex life. "It seems like we traded our friendship for kick-ass orgasms. And the truth is, the orgasms aren't worth it."

"Easy for you to say. Those of us who can't remember our last 'kick-ass orgasm' might feel differently." When Piper didn't respond, Gina sighed. "I hate to see you upset, but I'm not sure I can help."

"That's okay. Just talking about it has been helpful. I'm glad I told you." It had certainly been easier to admit her concerns to Gina than it would be to spell them out for Josh. Piper was afraid he wouldn't want to hear them.

But if he was too reticent to voice his feelings for her, assuming he had some, and she was too aware of the fate of his ex-lovers to broach the subject, what would keep their relationship from deteriorating to nothing more than cheap sex?

"I can't believe you made it this long without telling me the two of you have been hitting the sheets," Gina said. "I don't know whether I'm annoyed or impressed at your ability to keep a secret. But, Piper, it's not me you need to be having this conversation with. You've got to talk to *him*."

"I was afraid you were gonna say that."

As soon as Josh opened his door Friday evening, he understood that the moment he'd dreaded had arrived. One glance at Piper's face told him everything. She looked like a woman trying hard to appear nonchalant about something that was vitally important to her. And she looked unhappy. He wasn't making her happy.

Even back in Rebecca, he'd known he wasn't the

right guy, couldn't give her what she needed, but he'd foolishly hoped he could have everything, anyway.

"Hey, Piper. Come on in."

"Thanks." She flashed an unconvincing smile, and he thought about what a pair of actors they were. First with her family. Now, miserably, with each other.

Glancing away from her fake smile, he told himself he was no better. His voice was full of forced cheer. "I just got home from the office." He jerked his thumb over his shoulder to indicate the kitchen. "I was about to get a drink. You want one?"

"Sure. If it's no trouble."

Right. Because pouring a second soft drink was going to be the difficult part of this confrontation.

In the sanctuary of his kitchen, he clenched his fists, fighting the rising tide of impotent rage, the recognition that once again he was losing someone. He hadn't seen the end coming quite so clearly with Dana, but he'd acquired more practice in the last several years. His stomach rolled over, and he felt as though he was sixteen again, just hearing the news that the Wakefields were going to Europe. Without him. Well, he wasn't a boy anymore. If he was losing Piper, he would take it like a man.

He walked back into the living room, where she waited on the sofa. "Here you go." Settling his weight on the arm of the couch, he handed her one of the cold drinks.

"Thanks." She took the glass, but immediately placed it on the scuffed-up coffee table, an antique he'd bought at a garage sale with plans to restore. It was actually quite a nice piece, given some work, but people so easily threw away belongings.

"What brings you up here?" His edgy mood made his voice abrupt. His words weren't rude, but his tone was chilly. Already detached.

Her eyes widened, and she drew back almost imperceptibly. Some would have missed the slight motion, but Josh was already watching for signs of withdrawal. "Do I need a reason to come see you? Although, now that I think of it, we don't spend any time in your apartment."

It was easier to be in someone else's. Easier to leave someone else's. "No, you don't need a reason. But I think you have one."

"Fair enough." She wouldn't meet his gaze. "I wanted to talk to you. You remember when I asked you what we were going to do about work?" She looked up then, but he had trouble reading her expression. Or maybe he didn't want to understand what he saw there. "You suggested we wait and see if we were going to develop into anything."

"Are you upset about that? I told you it didn't come out the way—"

"Josh. I'm not here to pressure you or guilt you or complain about the way you worded something. You don't even have to tell me right now if we've 'developed.' But when do you think you might know?" She rose, fidgeting nervously with her hands. "I didn't like ignoring you at work these last two weeks and feeling as if we're having some illicit, sordid relationship."

He wanted to believe it was only the work situation bothering her, but he'd already met his quota of self-delusion for the month. "You say you're not pressuring me, but you sound like you're hinting at some sort of ultimatum." The best defense was a good offense.

Her angry glare wasn't as worrisome as the resigned expression that almost immediately replaced it. "You know what? Maybe I am. It's not fair to you to give you a timetable or try to force some kind of commitment, I admit. But it's not fair to me to keep going on like this."

He wanted to say "Like what?" but, dammit, he knew.

He'd been the one to close his eyes when she was staring deep into his because it had been the only way he knew to save his soul. He'd been the one who barely spoke to her at work, telling himself that it was professionalism, not fear. He'd been the one who left her after making love because holding her while she slept would just cement how much he loved her, something he dared not voice because he wanted to defend whatever tiny part of his heart could still be protected from her leaving.

She deserved more. So had the other women who had broken up with him for this very thing. *You never should have touched her*, he reminded himself. *You knew better.* She should be with a man capable of sharing his whole heart with someone. Josh feared he'd lost that ability somewhere between foster homes four and five. Or maybe five and six. Who could keep count? *Do the right thing and let her go.*

He was going to lose her, but he wasn't going to negotiate with her the way he had with Dana, attempting to find inside him whatever it was she wanted. Even if he said the right words today, they were only words. They wouldn't change who he was or what she needed. It was best if she left now, before this hurt him, either of them, any worse.

"I agree with you, Piper."

"You do?" She blinked, looking surprised and hopeful.

"We *shouldn't* go on like this. It isn't fair to you."

"Ah." The cautious hope flickered, and a light went out in her eyes. The quick understanding in her disappointed expression was testament to how well she knew him. "You mean we shouldn't go on, period."

"It's not that I don't...care about you."

"Oh, God, this is actually it, isn't it—the Josh Weber goodbye? The it's-not-you, it's-me, you-deserve-more, let's-still-be-friends brush-off you give all your women?"

Anger slammed through him, not at her but with himself. All his women? Piper thought she was one of a crowd, and it was his own fault she didn't know that he'd never loved anyone this way, probably never would again. But how could he convince her she was special, when he couldn't convince himself that he deserved her?

"Yeah. I guess that's my goodbye," he told her. A *real* goodbye. Despite the let's-still-be-friends comment she'd hurled at him, he couldn't stomach a superficial friendship like those he maintained with some former lovers. Not with Piper.

"You're unbelievable." She looked enraged, but hadn't made any move toward the door yet. Didn't she know the adhesive bandage approach was best—just rip it off fast and hard? Taking one's time only increased the pain. "I don't even rate my own special brush-off? After the week we had? No points for creative positions or being extra limber?"

Her furious tone didn't keep him from seeing the calculating gleam in her eye. By reducing what they'd shared to crass terms, she'd given him the chance to protest that it had meant more.

He needed her to get out. Now. Before he begged her not to leave him. Pleading hadn't stopped people from abandoning him before, and he was too old to try it now.

"It was great sex, Piper, but it was just sex."

He almost flinched for her. Josh had *never* said something like that to a woman, not even when it had just been sex.

Piper opened her mouth, probably to call him a liar or a bastard, both of which would have been true. But then she silently pivoted...and left him.

14

JUST SEX? Piper wanted to kick the crap out of someone—Josh, for instance—but figured she'd make do with a punishing exercise regimen instead. So she returned to her gym's weight room for the second time that day. Though rusty on breakup procedures, she guessed she was due to be back home now, crying her eyes out and stuffing her face with Chocomel bars. She preferred embracing her anger.

Stay mad as long as possible, she instructed herself while she increased the weight resistance for her leg curls. Because as soon as the anger started to taper off, the pain would probably obliterate her.

Just sex. The words didn't bother her. After studying him very closely, plus the emotions he'd tried to keep out of his expression, she was certain Josh knew exactly how special their connection had been. She suspected that very connection was why the king of cordial separations had ditched his usual finesse in favor of finality.

No, what bothered her was that he'd deliberately run her off, rid himself of another woman, another relationship. A conversation she'd had with Gina rang silently in Piper's ears.

"He's hell on female hearts. You know how many women I've seen him break up with?"

"Maybe because he hasn't met the right one?"

"Won't matter. Josh isn't going to let himself find the right one."

And Piper had been the right woman for him, she was sure of it. Just as he was the perfect man for her. *That's* why this hurt so much, not because of something stupid he'd said to get her to leave. After the childhood he'd had, one would think he'd grab at the chance for happiness. But she couldn't force him to accept her love if he was too scared to give them a chance.

He wasn't the only one afraid, her conscience reminded her. Piper had been walking on eggshells since the first time they'd made love. She'd wanted to talk but had found excuses to avoid it so that she wouldn't lose him.

My fear was justified. I did lose him.

Yeah. But if she looked at it that way, his fear was justified, too. He'd lost her.

That was his own damn fault...wasn't it?

He'd pushed her away, sure, but she'd let herself be pushed. Piper slowly brought her legs back into the starting position and leaned against the padded, black vinyl seat, confusion condensing into an excruciating headache behind her eyes. After a moment, she realized that the pounding anger that had driven her to the gym had receded. Time for those Chocomels now, she figured as she stood.

Maybe she'd call Daphne and try to sort this out. But by the time Piper reached the locker room to retrieve her purse, she'd discounted that idea. Daph might have good advice, but Piper was too miserable to talk to half of a happily married couple right now. Gina, then? No, Gina was a great listener, but as she'd pragmatically pointed out last time they'd spoken, she couldn't actually do anything about the situation.

Come to think of it, Piper had been entirely too willing to let someone else solve her problems. She'd put off instigating a real conversation with Josh, and even this evening when she'd finally gone to see him....

"Oh, hell!" Her exclamation of self-disgust drew curious stares from the employees at the check-in desk, but she ignored them as she walked out into the cool evening air.

She'd gone upstairs today looking for a way to get Josh to admit to his feelings, to connect with her emotionally, but she'd guarded her own feelings. The man had lost everyone he'd ever loved, starting with his parents—a relationship most people, including Piper, took for granted. Josh couldn't take love for granted, couldn't let himself trust it.

I should have given him a reason to trust.

Maybe she still could. It would have to be convincing, though. She couldn't just call him up and tell him she loved him and wasn't going anywhere. He wouldn't believe her.

She needed to do something that would make a statement he could have faith in. Something that would prove she wasn't so easy to get rid of, that she was sticking around. Something big.

PIPER TOOK A DEEP BREATH, raising her fist to knock on the door of her boss's office. At just after seven-thirty on Monday morning, none of the other draftsmen had come in yet. Maria was here already to brew coffee and read the paper in the empty break room, but mostly, the place was deserted. It was a well-known fact, though, that Callahan, the founder of C, K and M, often put in early hours and was even here most weekends. Piper wanted to talk to the man before anyone else got to work.

"Come in." Callahan's gravelly voice was booming even through the door. She supposed someone who didn't know him might find him intimidating, but he'd always been her favorite of the three partners.

"Good morning, Mr. Callahan," she said as she entered the office.

"Piper." His bushy eyebrows arched upward. "You're here early today."

"I needed to speak to you, sir." She still couldn't believe she was quitting her job over a man. It was the complete opposite of what anyone would expect from her, but that's exactly why she thought it might penetrate Josh's thick skull. Or the thick barriers around his heart. She loved him enough to leave C, K and M, solving the fraternization problem, if she could convince him to fraternize again.

And if she couldn't...well, working here and having him banter meaninglessly with her the way he did with Nancy from Grazzio's would be unbearable.

"Please, have a seat," Callahan invited.

She glanced at the two straight-back chairs available, but she was feeling too restless and edgy to sit down. "Actually, if you don't mind, I'll stand. Might make this easier. Sir, I've enjoyed working for C, K and M." A what-the-hell-I'm-quitting-anyway brand of honesty allowed her to add, "Well, working for you, at least. But I've given this a lot of thought over the weekend, and I'm afraid I have to turn in my resignation."

He leaned back in his office chair, regarding her silently for a long moment. Nervousness made her feel a little shaky, and she regretted not having sat down.

"I see. I'm sorry to hear it, of course. Do you mind if I ask if this is the result of anything one of the partners has done, or could have done differently?"

"No, sir. I'm leaving for personal reasons."

"That's a shame. You're one of my most promising employees...and C, K and M will be shorthanded now that Mr. Weber has quit, too."

Well, that did it. She sank into the nearest chair. "Josh quit? When?" Had he arrived at six-thirty instead of seven o'clock? After mulling this over for the past two days, she'd thought she'd calculated her exit perfectly.

By the time Josh arrived at work today, she figured she could tell him she was leaving and it would be too late for him to talk her out of it. She could also tell him that her feelings weren't going to disappear because of an argument they'd had in his apartment, that he should call her if he was ever ready for a real relationship and the emotional risks it entailed.

Only Josh wasn't coming into work today, she realized.

"He stopped by on Saturday," Callahan said. "Told me that those sideline jobs have grown plentiful enough that he's going into business for himself, and he hopes there aren't hard feelings. I hate to lose him, but I remember what it was like to want to make a name for myself. His workload must be impressive, because he made his resignation effective immediately."

She knew Callahan was studying her, but she couldn't lift her gaze from her lap. It felt too heavy. Everything felt heavy. "I suppose he thought a clean, quick break would be best."

Josh had run away. From her, from what they could have together. It wasn't the same thing she was trying to do at all. She half wondered if he was making plans to move out of their building. *Why did I think I could make this work?* On the plus side, he'd never cared enough to run from previous relationships. He'd been very casual about his breakups until now. She felt herself smile for the first time that morning.

"Well, I'm happy to give you two weeks," she told Callahan. In fact, it gave her more time to make phone calls. She'd picked up business cards and interested contacts over the years and had plenty in savings to get by for a couple of months, but it wasn't as though she had a brand-new job lined up yet. "After that, I can wrap up a few things from home if you need it."

"Can I make a counteroffer, Piper? Why don't you take a personal day, maybe two, and reconsider? As a favor to me. You started out at the appropriate level here at C, K and M, but maybe we didn't advance you as quickly as we should have. Your review is coming up soon, or was, and I had planned to increase your leadership responsibilities then. Perhaps I should have done so before now."

He was making her a project manager. She'd wanted this, but she wanted Josh to share it with even more. "I...my quitting was not an attempt to force your hand, sir."

He nodded. "I understand."

She rather feared he did, and tears pricked her eyes, making her blink. All this energy she'd put into her job, all the times she'd insisted she didn't need or want a man in her life. No wonder they said be careful what you wished for.

In the end, Piper did accept a personal day to rethink her decision. Given what she'd learned about Josh in her meeting with Callahan, it made considerably less sense to leave C, K and M, but she could use some time to clear her head. Driving back to her apartment, she reevaluated her other plans, as well. Should she still try to convince Josh of her feelings?

Yes. If she didn't, she'd be letting fear control her as much as he was letting his past control him. She'd talk to him, but not today. It wasn't even 9:00 a.m. when she stepped back inside her apartment, but she already felt as if she'd been put through the emotional wringer.

After taking a restless nap on her couch and watching some really bad afternoon television, which almost made her feel better about her own life, Piper decided she'd wallowed enough. Since she had some unexpected free time, she might as well use it for something besides looking around her apartment at the places she and Josh had made love during their brief but intense relationship.

Silencing a distraught soap opera grande dame with a well-aimed remote control, Piper rose from the sofa. Laundry was a top priority; she'd been going through workout clothes faster than normal lately. Then maybe a trip to the grocery store. She was also going through a lot of Chocomel bars since she'd been home. After she'd gathered a hamper of clothes and a pen and pad to make a shopping list, she walked out to the elevator in her socks.

As she approached the laundry room, she heard the rhythmic rumble of a dryer. She turned the corner, and her heart stopped at the sight of Josh sitting in one of the blue plastic chairs. His shoulders were slumped, and he was running a hand through his hair. Not for the first time, judging by the unkempt furrows in the dark mass. Yet he still looked heartbreakingly sexy, she thought, her eyes sliding from his strong, achingly familiar profile to his leanly muscled torso and the denim-clad legs stretched out in front of him.

He straightened as soon as he realized he wasn't alone, turning toward her with a friendly smile that was replaced by a much more sincere look of shock when he saw it was her. "Piper! What are you doing here?"

Josh couldn't believe his eyes. He'd been thinking of her nonstop since he'd last seen her Friday evening, and now she was standing there as though she'd simply walked out of his imagination. Except in not one of his mental images had she been balancing a white clothes hamper against her hip and scowling at him.

"You thought I'd be at the office." She made it an accusation.

"Well, it is the middle of the day on Monday." Which was precisely why he was here now. He'd solved the seeing-her-at-work problem, and figured with some effort to avoid her in the building, they could both live in the same apartment complex for a while. "Why *aren't* you at the office?"

She stepped forward, dropping her hamper on a low table with an angry thud. "Same reason you aren't. I quit."

Regret pooled inside him, churning in his stomach. Not only had he been a jerk, he'd screwed up her job for her. "You shouldn't quit. You don't need to quit. I—"

"Beat me to it. Yeah, that's what Callahan said. I

don't know why I was even surprised. You leave relationships, you leave my apartment, you leave the company."

He managed not to flinch at the reproach in her voice. "All for the best."

She snorted, hands planted on her hips. Any other time, her feisty demeanor might have made him smile. "It's not for the best. It's nuts, you know that? This could be great. *We* could be great."

For a second, he was too stunned to say anything. He'd hardly expected her to speak to him again, much less argue in favor of their being together. Was there a chance she still wanted him, a chance he could give her what she needed if she did take him back? He squelched the unexpected hope before it could hurt someone.

But he couldn't squelch Piper. She narrowed her eyes and made a decidedly unromantic vow of affection. "I love you, you idiot, and I'm pretty sure you could love me if you'd stop screwing this up for both of us."

I love you. Though some part of him had known how she felt, her declaration rattled him nonetheless. He'd known Piper didn't take sex or their friendship lightly, and while maybe their night in Rebecca could have "just happened," she never would have continued with their fling if she didn't have very strong feelings for him. But it had been a long time since anyone had actually said those words to him, even longer since someone had truly meant it.

She was right about his feelings, too. He'd probably started falling in love with her the night he'd moved into his apartment and had encountered her in this very room, dancing to a rock ballad on the radio while her darks were on spin cycle.

"Piper, I—"

"No." She held up her hand. "I let you say things that weren't true on Friday, let you push me away, and I'm not giving you that chance again. You're not pushing me away now, Josh. I'm leaving of my own accord so that you don't do the guy thing and say more stupid stuff you can't take back. Just think about this, okay? Think about what it would be like to finally have something that lasts with someone who loves you."

Without even pausing to collect her clothes, she pivoted and marched toward the doorway, and he knew what her hurry was. He'd heard the tremor in her voice and hated himself for any tears he'd caused her. But the shakiness with which she'd spoken didn't mask her conviction in what she was saying, a bone-deep certainty he envied. He didn't think he'd ever let himself be sure of anything he couldn't control, never let himself trust in an emotion that completely.

She'd offered him love that lasted. Was it really within his grasp?

That dark voice inside started to tell him no, of course not, but Josh shut it out. He'd shied away from hope and clung to fear, and where had it landed him? Alone and miserable without Piper. A future of missing her stretched before him.

You couldn't do anything about your past. But you can do something about this.

And if he didn't, then she was right. He was an idiot.

JOSH STEPPED OFF the elevator and into the hall, but the walk to Piper's front door had never seemed so long. It was almost comical how hard his heart was thudding against his chest. How many times over the last two years had he traced this very same path? She'd told him a mere hour ago that she loved him, so why was he still so scared?

Because maybe she's come to her senses by now.

He ignored the pessimistic thought and knocked on her door. "Piper, it's me, Josh."

After the way he'd behaved, he wouldn't have blamed her if she refused to answer. If all else failed, maybe he could ransom the hamper full of clothes she'd abandoned in exchange for her hearing him out. But she opened the door, swinging it wide with a wary expression on her face. She was dressed the same as she had been earlier—ponytail, sweatpants, T-shirt. Somehow the contrast between the nondescript clothes and her own beauty made her even sexier than if she'd been wearing something obviously attractive.

"You really are beautiful." That hadn't been how he'd planned to start the conversation, but how could he go wrong with an opener like that?

"If you came down here with empty flattery, I'll break a vase over your head." But she sounded more uncertain than her bravado implied. She was trying to decide why he was here at all, and not quite allowing herself to hope. He knew the feeling.

"There was nothing empty about what I said. Can I come in?" He held out the green-cellophane-wrapped cone. "I would have been here sooner, but I wanted to get you these."

She glanced at the clusters of baby breath peeking out. "Flowers?"

"Not exactly."

She looked down inside the wrapping and laughed. He wondered if she'd ever seen a Chocomel bouquet before. It had certainly been a first for the surprised florist.

"I figured it was a good start toward groveling for forgiveness." His body tightened as he recalled playfully seeking her forgiveness on their first date, making love with her in her kitchen. He'd like nothing more than the physical reassurance of holding her close and making love now. But they had to talk first.

Glancing up from the bouquet to meet his gaze, Piper smiled. "I love you."

He didn't think he'd ever get used to hearing it. "I—" Paralyzing fear gripped him, but it wasn't as strong as what he felt for this woman. The words had gone unsaid too long. "I love you, too."

Her expression blossomed, full of tenderness and radiant joy. The Chocomels fell to the floor as she moved forward to wrap her arms around his neck. She pulled him closer and proceeded to kiss him breathless.

Stepping inside her apartment without breaking the kiss, Josh nudged the door closed behind them. He nipped her lower lip, but then angled his head away from hers. "We have to stop."

"Maybe we should take a vote on that," Piper told him, nibbling the side of his neck.

Need trembled through him. She had to know it was about more than just the sex, though. "We can vote just as soon as we've talked."

Her arms slid to her sides as she glanced up at him in shock. "Really? You'd rather talk?" She didn't look so much disappointed as optimistic, and he was reminded of how badly he'd botched things up during the past week. He was also reminded of everything he wanted. Love. Commitment. All the things he'd been afraid to hope for, but that now seemed possible with Piper beside him.

"Yeah. You deserve to know how you make me feel." He took her hand, leading her over to the sofa, determined to get it all out before he regressed. "I know you just needed someone for the weekend, Piper, but... You know better than anyone that I wasn't looking for someone to share my life, but over the last two years, you've become so important to me. I can't really imagine you not being there in the years to come. Actually, I *can*. That's what I've been doing the last few days, and it's been awful."

She squeezed his hand, but didn't say anything, and he took the silent encouragement to go on. He wanted to be with her, but she should know what she was getting.

"I love you—I can't believe how good it feels to finally say it—but I'm probably going to screw this up in dozens of ways."

Her voice was thick with unshed tears. "Then you'll make it up to me in dozens more. Josh, I know you. You're kind and giving and passionate. You have more capacity to love than you think."

Her faith in him was humbling. He framed his face with her hands. "Maybe you just bring it out in me." He leaned forward to kiss her, his body raging with the need to show her physically how much he cherished her. But he stopped himself, worried about one other thing and determined not to rush into sex just because it was so much easier than talking. "I'll support your decision if it's what you really want to do, but I wish you hadn't quit your job. Not because of me."

He'd quit for the wrong reasons initially, but the fact of the matter was he looked forward to the challenge of building his own business. Piper, on the other hand, had been determined to prove herself at C, K and M and had done good work there. He hated that she'd left.

Leaning forward, she brushed her lips against his in what was less a kiss and more a promise of things to come. "Don't worry. Callahan and I are negotiating for me to return. I might even get a raise out of this, so you did me a favor." She shot Josh a sheepish smile. "Speaking of past favors... You're prepared to deal with my family in order to be with me?"

"I love your nutty relatives almost as much as I love you." He touched his tongue to the soft spot just below her earlobe, and she shivered. "You think you can handle my not being used to sharing my emotions with anyone?"

"Don't worry. You'll get better with practice, and I'm not giving up on you."

Not giving up on him. God, he loved her.

She ran her hand underneath the hem of his shirt, her fingers skimming up his chest, resting near his heart. "You're okay with the fact that I can barely cook anything besides chocolate chip pancakes and lasagna?"

"That's what take-out's for," he answered, loving her touch against his skin. "You should be aware, I'm pretty certain I snore."

"Worth it to have you in my bed," she assured him.

He pulled her closer, lifting her from the couch to

straddle his lap, groaning at the friction of her sweet, sexy weight atop him. Their mouths met, and he'd never been more hungry for a kiss, wanting to greedily lap up every joy this woman could bring to his life. Wanting to give her the same joy.

She pulled back slightly, her smile as full of mischief as it was adoration. "So would *now* be a good time to vote on whether or not we should make love? All in favor—"

"Aye."

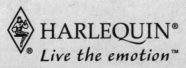

If you enjoyed what you just read,
then we've got an offer you can't resist!

Take 2 bestselling
love stories FREE!
Plus get a FREE surprise gift!

Clip this page and mail it to Harlequin Reader Service®

IN U.S.A.	IN CANADA
3010 Walden Ave.	P.O. Box 609
P.O. Box 1867	Fort Erie, Ontario
Buffalo, N.Y. 14240-1867	L2A 5X3

YES! Please send me 2 free Harlequin Temptation® novels and my free surprise gift. After receiving them, if I don't wish to receive anymore, I can return the shipping statement marked cancel. If I don't cancel, I will receive 4 brand-new novels each month, before they're available in stores. In the U.S.A., bill me at the bargain price of $3.57 plus 25¢ shipping and handling per book and applicable sales tax, if any*. In Canada, bill me at the bargain price of $4.24 plus 25¢ shipping and handling per book and applicable taxes**. That's the complete price and a savings of 10% off the cover prices—what a great deal! I understand that accepting the 2 free books and gift places me under no obligation ever to buy any books. I can always return a shipment and cancel at any time. Even if I never buy another book from Harlequin, the 2 free books and gift are mine to keep forever.

142 HDN DNT5
342 HDN DNT6

Name	(PLEASE PRINT)	
Address	Apt.#	
City	State/Prov.	Zip/Postal Code

* Terms and prices subject to change without notice. Sales tax applicable in N.Y.
** Canadian residents will be charged applicable provincial taxes and GST.
   All orders subject to approval. Offer limited to one per household and not valid to current Harlequin Temptation® subscribers.
® are registered trademarks of Harlequin Enterprises Limited.

TEMP02   ©1998 Harlequin Enterprises Limited

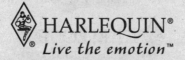